L ROSE

PROTECTED

BY THE FOX SHIFTER

Strawberrys.art

For the readers who enjoy little murderous fox shifters that will do anything for you.

TRIGGER WARNINGS

Blood, violence, kidnapping, hate (homophobic) slurs, sexual content. BDSM with a daddy/boy relationship

BLURB

Riker

I'm younger than my brothers, wilder, and I relish the hunt of a kill in my fox and human forms more than either of them. But I'm also the cutest shifter there is. Everyone loves me, so obviously my fated mate will have no choice but to fall for me.

Even if I have to make him.

Corbin

I'm still trying to work out why I felt compelled to rescue the guy—who I can't seem to take my eyes off—from that damn beast that looked set on killing him. What I don't expect is to hear the energizer bunny incarnate telling me he's mine forever.

I can see he walks to his own beat, but I kinda like the idea of keeping him.

Making him mine.

Hell, I'm already looking forward to seeing what my MC brothers will think of the murderous twink when I bring him into the clubhouse.

PROLOGUE

(FROM KIERAN'S POV IN THE PREVIOUS NOVELLA: PROTECTED BY THE TIGER SHIFTER)

Deacon roared in his shifted bear form before he and Nox stalked toward their brother.

A gun cocked off to the side.

Everyone stilled when a man in dark jeans, biker boots, and a leather vest over a dark tee walked out from the shadows. In the hand that had tattoos on it was a gun pointed at Deacon's bear.

"Don't fuckin' move," he ordered, gaze wild, breathing heavy.

"Who are you?" Soren called.

The guy ignored him and walked right up to Riker. Deacon took a step. The gun fired, and a chair behind Deacon's bear fell to the floor in a clatter.

"Move again and the next bullet will be in your brain." He wound an arm around Riker's waist and, since the guy was a lot taller, he picked Riker up before moving step by step backward.

The bear growled.

Nox took a step toward them. "You're not taking—"

"Don't ruin my kidnapping, Nox," Riker said with a manic grin. He patted the kidnapper's arm before he waved at us all. "Don't worry about me." He winked. "This must be *fate*."

Well, heck. Riker had just met his fated mate, who was currently kidnapping him for some reason. Then again, he could be human and acting on instinct alone after witnessing a man change into a bear. A bear that looked like he was going to kill Riker.

Sighing, I scrubbed a hand over my face. He'd be okay. And he could take care of himself.

CHAPTER ONE

CORBIN

*W*hat in the motherfucking hell did I just witness? A man morphed into a damn bear. A big, brown grizzly bear. It'd been right there before my fucking eyes.

All because of the deep nagging feeling in my chest that had me staying in the nightclub—even after the alarm had sounded getting everyone else out—to save the guy who was practically vibrating in the seat next to me in the car.

Christ. What was I doing kidnapping this guy?

I glanced out of the corner of my eye and then tightened my grip around the steering wheel when my cock thickened. He'd been biting down on his plump bottom lip yet smiling around it.

I'd never seen hair that orange, where it nearly damn glowed, and his amber eyes were so fucking bright. His smooth skin called to me, and I wanted to run the back of my fingers over the globes of his cheeks just to test how soft they were.

The only problem was how small he was. Short and skinny, yet when I picked him up to carry him out of the club, he was slim but toned.

Jesus Christ.

Why the fuck was I even checking him out and thinking about how toned he was to begin with?

I'd never admired a man before, but I'd never considered it before either. Until now. Until my interest was piqued by this ball of energy at my side.

The guy sat on his hands, but his legs bounced up and down. He kept looking at me and grinning like a madman.

Fuck me. What was I supposed to do with him now?

"You got a place to go?"

"Nope." Another wide grin beamed my way.

"A home? Family?" I tried.

"I'm good here."

Fucking hell.

"Look, I had to get you out of there. That fuckin' guy changed into a real live bear. You ever see any shit like that before?"

"Yep." He nodded.

On autopilot, I pulled into my driveway.

Why did I bring him here?

I should have taken him to the compound, not my private place.

Hell, I should have dropped him off on the side of the road. I'd done my job getting him out of there since it was clear those two guys were going to kill him.

Actually, what was more important, was to figure out how I got home without even thinking. I just acted on instinct. Snorting to myself, I shook my head. I headed to a place of comfort, my mind buzzing with what I fucking saw.

A guy changed into a bear.

A fucking bear.

Hang on... did he say yes?

Switching off the ignition, I faced him, and even though the cabin was dark, the outside light spilled light through the car's windows. "Did you say you've seen somethin' like that before?"

He wiggled in the seat until he faced my way, nodding. "I did."

Scrubbing a hand over my face, I sighed. "I'm not sure I want to know."

"It's best you do."

Fuck.

What did I get myself into?

Drawing in a deep breath, I pushed my door open and stepped out into the evening air. Since we were here, we might as well head inside for this conversation. The young guy rushed from the car after me.

Hell, I didn't even know what to call him.

At the front door, I asked, "Name?"

"Riker Blackwood. What's yours? I can't keep calling you 'the hottest man I've ever seen.' Though, I still might do it in my mind even after you tell me your name. That's if you don't mind. Do you mind?"

Slowly, and before we entered since I wasn't sure having him in my house was good, I gave Riker all my attention.

He rocked on his feet with his hands clasped behind his back and a smile still in place.

This little twink thought I was handsome?

I was old enough to be his daddy.

He seemed early twenties. I was at least double that at forty-two.

Still, I pushed those thoughts aside and instead asked, "Do you usually say what's on your mind?"

"Uh-huh. I sure do." He thinned his lips, and I was damn positive it was to stop himself from saying more. He squirmed a little and then blurted, "Your name?"

Shit. I wanted to laugh. My lips even twitched, but I forced them into a frown, confused by my attraction and attention to this guy.

"Razor."

His stunning gaze dropped from my face to my cut, or the patch on my cut, then up again.

God, he was short. The top of his head was at my collarbone.

"Razor? That's your club name. I can see it there." He pointed to the patch. "And that you're the president to the Fury motorcycle club. But what's your birth name?"

"Corbin."

Why the fuck did I tell him? No one knew unless they were important to me, and yet, there I was, spewing it out to this Riker guy I kidnapped.

Ignoring the way he lit up after hearing it, I demanded, "Why the fuck are you still here? I stole you, kid."

He bounced on his feet again, holding his hands together under his chin. "But you did it to save me."

"Christ," I grumbled. "I ain't no hero, so don't even fuckin' think that shit. Those two pricks back there were lookin' for your blood. I took you out of the situation and that's it. Actually, you can leave now." I waved him off.

Jesus motherfucking Christ. The way he looked at me, like I'd gutted him right there on my front porch, stabbed *me* right in the heart.

Closing my eyes, I tipped my head back and asked for... I didn't have a clue what to ask for. *Patience? A head exam? Help for things to make sense?*

Grumbling some curse words, I turned, unlocked the door, and flung it wide before I reached in to turn on the living room light.

Moving out of the way, I ordered, "Get inside."

His playful puppy look was back in full force. "Okay," he sang as he bounced through. "We have so much to talk about, and I can't wait until I show you what I can do. You didn't freak out over Deacon. You just strolled up with your gun raised high—like a wet dream—while you demanded them not to move so you could grab me right out from there. Which was awesome, by the way." He made his way around the living room, looking and touching everything he saw. "This is pretty," he said, picking up a dagger my pops, the last living relative who passed five years ago—God rest his soul—gave me when I took over the club after my dickhead of a father overdosed.

I wouldn't exactly call a dagger pretty, but as I watched Riker pick it up gently to twist it this way and that, I noticed he really was admiring it as if it was something wondrous. He ran his thumb over the sharp edge.

"Careful," I barked, stomping over and taking his hand away. Blood already welled. Instinctively, I put his digit in my mouth and sucked.

Then froze.

Until my gaze traveled to Riker's. His pupils were blown wide, and he bit his bottom lip.

Swiftly, I removed his thumb and shoved his hand away to stalk across the room.

I had to keep my distance from the boy.

He appealed to me too much and all in a matter of moments. No one had ever done that. Hell, I'd even got an excited dip to my gut from how Riker looked ready to cut himself again while wanting me to fuck him senseless.

And how I got that visual all from a single look, I had no clue.

My cock ached and throbbed like I was a teen again.

Why this boy?

The metallic taste of his blood lingered in my mouth no matter how many times I swallowed. It made me want to bite him again to see that heat in his stunning gaze.

Mark him up in punishment.

I unlocked my jaw and ordered sharply, "Sit the fuck down."

I was pissed at him, pissed at myself, and pissed about the whole situation.

Hell, maybe it was just my confusion turned into annoyance.

I didn't fucking know.

He swayed his hips over to the couch and sat in the corner, leaning back, totally relaxed. Like he wasn't in a stranger's house where anything could happen.

I could kill him for fuck's sake.

I sat on the chair opposite him and planted my feet up on the wooden chest, which I used as a table, between us. While I looked just as relaxed as he did, on the inside, it was a different story. Confusion, desire, and anger blended together. I didn't quite trust the guy since he was willing to walk in here without a care. But at least where I sat, there was a gun stuffed down the side of my chair.

Placing my hands over my gut, I demanded, "Talk."

A wicked grin slowly tugged up his goddamn kissable lips.

Kissable? I should just shoot myself now. He's a kid, dickhead.

"I can talk about lots of things. What would you like me to talk about? How I know you liked the way you sucked off my blood, but I wished you were sucking off—"

"Shut the fuck up," I snarled, planting my feet on the floor to sit forward.

He cackled before he kicked off his shoes and crossed his legs up on the couch.

What the fuck?

Who was this guy and why didn't he feel any fear?

He scraped his top teeth over his bottom lip. He knew he had my full attention.

"Sorry, I'll be good." He winked. "Well, I'll *try* to. What did you want to know first?"

"You said you'd seen something like that guy becoming a bear before. Start there."

He saluted me. "You got it, Sir."

I ground my teeth together as arousal slammed into me.

Riker's face tipped up as he sniffed the air, his pupils expanded.

"What's up with your eyes?"

"Nah-ah-ah, that's for another time. Maybe soon. Maybe not." He shrugged.

Fuck me. What was with this guy?

He wiggled in his spot. "You wanted an answer to your first question, so I'll do that. The man who morphed into a bear is a shifter. The man beside him is another, but a tiger."

Holy motherfucking hell.

Two *shifters.*

A bear and a tiger. Who would have thought that shit was real? Not me. But there was no denying what I saw when it'd been thrown in my face.

I blinked.

"Wait, you know them?"

"I do."

I ground my teeth together. How could he seem so blasé? "They were going to kill you," I clipped, wondering why I cared so much about a guy I knew nothing of.

Riker shrugged again.

Fucking hell, he definitely had a screw loose.

He brushed invisible lint off his jeans and glared down

at them like the material had offended him. He looked back up and smiled over at me. "They would've only *harmed* me. Not killed. They'd never kill me."

"How can you be certain? And why the fuck were you just standing there waiting for those guys, *who changed into animals*, to *harm* you?"

"Because."

Growling out my frustration, I stood and crossed my arms over my chest. "Can you give me a straight fuckin' answer without the dance around?"

He beamed. "I like dancing."

I used one hand to rub at my temples. My thumb and two fingers circled the points where a headache formed.

Sighing, I tried again, "Riker, please tell me how you knew they wouldn't kill you."

"Okay, Corbin. By the way, I like your name. I know because they're my brothers. The bear is Deacon, and the tiger is Nox."

Dropping my hand, I stared at him.

"Your brothers?"

"Yep." He nodded and bounced around until he was kneeling on the couch.

"Bullshit. You look nothing alike."

"Foster brothers," he said like it explained everything.

I had a feeling he wasn't being forthcoming with everything because he liked this game of back and forth.

Or he just liked me. He'd already made that obvious.

But....

"Does that mean you change into an animal?"

Where in the fuck was my life going?

I didn't want to believe this. I didn't want to even know about it. The information was damn wild.

"Yes. I'm a fox shifter."

"Prove it," I commanded.

"Okay," he said happily as he jumped from the couch. He pulled off his tee and started on his pants.

"What're you doin'?"

Riker paused with his fingers on his zipper. "Undressing."

"Why?"

"Oh, so I don't get caught up in my clothes. Sometimes they tear too."

"This is real. You're actually going to change into an animal?"

"Yeah, Corbin."

Christ, I liked the way my name sounded on his lips.

"Fuck," I clipped and nodded.

When he grinned again, I wondered if he ever stopped with his sunshine attitude?

He shoved his jeans and underwear down. Then he paused with his hands on his hips, displaying himself for me and, I admit, I looked.

I drank in every fucking inch of his pale, silky skin. I shouldn't, but I didn't have the strength to look away, and it wasn't like he was hiding himself. He stood proudly while I admired.

My cock jerked in my jeans. Hell, even my balls felt heavy. A need to be inside him punched me in the lower gut.

Who the fuck was this guy?

When I dragged my attention back to his face, I sucked in a sharp breath as his bones broke. They reshaped as fur sprouted before he, somehow, shrunk down to a damn fox.

He hadn't been lying.

I sat my ass down on the chair behind me. In fact, if it hadn't been there, I would have hit the floor since my knees gave out on me.

"Jesus Christ," I uttered, staring at the fox from where it sat panting with his tongue hanging out the side of his mouth.

It was the cutest damn thing I'd seen.

But he'd been a man.

Only seconds ago.

The fox rose and danced around in a circle, chasing its tail. It drew out an unexpected laugh from me, but I slammed my lips closed and thinned them.

The fox had heard, though. He stopped its game to walk toward me.

I stilled as it grew closer. I didn't know what it'd do.

My body jolted at the chittering noise it made before he licked at my hand that I rested on my thigh.

He licked again, then nudged it with his nose.

It couldn't want a pat, right?

Fuck, I wanted to try anyway.

"Just don't bite my hand off," I told him.

He chittered louder while prancing from side to side on its paws.

Seemed both parts, animal and human, had similar traits. This fox couldn't keep still.

Reaching out, I ran my palm over its head. He pushed

up into it and shivered as I glided it down over his soft back.

In a blink, the fox was a man.

Riker tipped his head back and smirked up at me. "You can pat me anytime and anywhere."

CHAPTER TWO

RIKER

My mate let out a manly yelp and, unfortunately, removed his hand from my back as he jolted away. But at least his movement sent a whiff of his scent into my nose. I took in a big lungful. It reminded me of savoring a mug of warm chocolate milk in the deepest part of a forest while hunting for prey.

Hmm, yum. But would my mate even like hot chocolate? I had to search his cupboards to see if he had any chocolate at all. I liked Rio's chocolate muffins and cookies. He made the best ones.

"What the fuck, Riker," Corbin bit out.

I kneeled at his feet. A position I wouldn't mind doing anytime he asked, or demanded, or forced.

Yeah, I would like to see his tattooed hand—tatts that also ran up his arm, just the one because he was the coolest guy I'd ever met—grip the back of my neck and force me to the floor to take his stiff cock into my mouth until I choked on it.

"Why the fuck are you hard?" he growled.

I grinned, slowly running my tongue out over my lips as I watched my mate's stern eyes follow it.

The scent of arousal kept coming and going. Right then, it was strong and intense, and I could get drunk off it. I wanted to lean back to grip my prick and jerk off while he stared.

No, no. I wanted to lean into him and brush my face over his crotch to see if he was as erect as I was, and then I could sneak his zipper down and swallow around his hardness. He would be firm. I mean, I was naked in front of him.

"My dick likes you and the position I'm in." I flicked my gaze to his crotch and back up.

He ground his teeth together. "Fuckin' hell, you shouldn't talk shit like that."

I cocked my head to the side. "Why not?"

He stilled when he felt my fingers walking up his leg.

"Riker," he warned.

"Hmm?" I tried for a sweet smile and innocent eyes.

I was positive he didn't mind what I was saying and doing since another wave of his desire slammed into me. Stronger. Headier. Besides, he hadn't punched me for my teasing actions.

He shook his leg out and glowered. "Quit it."

"Why?" I whined. It didn't make sense. My mouth already watered at the thought of having his dick in it.

He sighed and rubbed at his temples before running

his palm over his face. Another glare followed. "How old are you?"

"Thirty-six."

A bark of laughter left him, but he cut it off quickly, which had me pouting. I liked his laugh. It was deep and rough like his voice. I wanted to hear more of it. I could tickle him. But if he wasn't ticklish, it was likely he'd get irritated with me like Nox and Deacon did every time I tried to get them to laugh when they were being a pain.

"Bullshit," my mate accused.

"Nuh-uh," I said.

I rolled up to my feet and paused for a moment so he could look at my amazing hard dick again. Then I walked over to my jeans and took out my wallet. Of course, my ID was forged since Blackwood was Deacon's last name. Nox and I changed ours to his when we were younger, so we all matched. But my mate wouldn't know it was fake.

At least it did show my actual age.

I looked younger. I took after my mother apparently. But she was killed soon after I was born when the monster saw how small I was and presumed I wouldn't be alpha enough.

I showed him, though. I showed all of them.

The memory conjured up the image of their dead bodies on the living room floor of my childhood house. I'd had blood on every inch of my six-year-old body. Even in my mouth and teeth. I'd fought them in animal and human forms, changing back and forth quickly. That was when they'd discovered I was the fastest in the pack at shifting.

Four bodies had lain lifeless on the carpet.

A father. An uncle. A grandfather. And a cousin.

All who had tormented my tiny body and soul.

"Hey."

I blinked, focusing on my wallet in my hand before I drew my gaze up to my mate who stood in front of me.

He pinched my chin and tilted my head back a little more, maybe so he could keep my eyes on his. "You okay?"

"Yep." I grinned. I hadn't been good seconds ago with those thoughts. But I now was. Yes, I was very good because he was touching me. My fated was concerned for me. I wanted to reach up to brush my finger over his pinched brows, but I didn't.

I needed to slow my wooing down. I didn't want to scare him, and I was pretty good at pursuing.

At least, I was pretty sure I had to slow down. I'd wait and see.

If he fisted my cock right then, I wouldn't stop him.

"Where did your head go?" he asked.

I slumped my shoulders when I guessed we weren't getting handsy and he was talking about why I spaced before.

"In the past."

He grunted. "Didn't look fun."

I shrugged. He wouldn't be ready to hear what I'd done.

What happened if he couldn't love me?

Fear gripped my throat, even as I stared up at him as his eyes roamed over my face.

Please love me. Love me like no one else. Love me like you can't live without me because I'll be doing the same for you.

He removed his fingers from my chin and coldness seeped in.

Corbin took my wallet from my hand and ordered, "Put your jeans on."

Boo. Even my fox released an annoyed chitter of disappointment.

I liked being naked. It was freeing and reminded me of my fox in his form with no restriction on his body.

However, I liked my mate more, as did my fox, and we wanted him to be comfortable.

While I slipped into my jeans, I watched him open my wallet and pull my license from it. His jaw clenched as he read it, eyes narrowing.

"Is this real?"

"The only thing fake is my last name. I'm really thirty-six. Ask my brothers. Ask my foster mom, who's also a shifter. A wolf. You'll love her, but not too much. Not more than me."

He snorted. "Why would I love you?"

Why wouldn't he? I was a catch.

Unless he wasn't gay or bi. Oh, he'd better not have a woman.

"Riker?"

"What?" I snapped, anger from the thought of him already in a relationship hardening the word.

"Now where's your head gone? Fuck me, it's like I'm on a roller coaster or havin' a bad trip. Only I haven't done that shit in twenty years."

Laughing, I reached out and patted his arm. Then I stared at his arm before I curled both hands around his bicep and grinned when he flexed it.

"You done touching me up now?" he asked with humor in his lighter tone.

"No. I could go all night long."

"Riker—"

"*All night*, Corbin. I'd be better than any other woman or man."

He chuckled and shook his head. "Christ, what the fuck, kid?"

"I may look like a kid, but this kid has stamina. You could pound my ass all the time and I'd still come back for more because I love cock in my ass, my mouth—"

"Shut your mouth," he snarled, cupping the side of my neck and dragging me close.

"Oh, I like this." I grinned up at him as I ran my hands over his chest under his vest.

"Why do I want to fuck you?" He asked in a way that told me he'd never thought about fucking a guy before.

Goody, I'm gonna be his first.

Hip hip hooray!

Even my dick was singing its own tune since it already ached that much.

"I'm fuckable," I told him. "But once you have my ass, you'll have to keep me forever."

"It's not only me wanting to be in you. There's something about you that.... Fucked if I know. It calls to me. Any other time I wouldn't put up with someone jumping from one thing to another. I'd either make them talk, and not in a pleasant way, or get rid of them. But you, even when it drives me crazy, I'm willing to wait and see what else comes out of your mouth next."

I winked. "I guess I'm just that lucky guy."

"Not sure if it's luck, Riker."

It was luck and fate, but I wouldn't tell him just yet. Maybe soon. I'd see where this would go. *If* he picked me. *Wanted* me. Though, it was hard to focus when I had his mouth this close. A shadow of stubble surrounded a mouth that I very much wanted to kiss and nibble at. I didn't mind either way. I'd even take a lick if he gave me the chance. What would it look like wrapped around *my* cock? Would he give head if he'd never been with a guy?

I couldn't believe he was already admitting he wanted to fuck me.

His honesty was refreshing.

Concentrate, Riker.

What are we talking about?

Oh, right. He wasn't sure if him wanting me was luck on my part. "Why?"

His jaw clenched. "Don't know yet." His eyes locked onto his hand at the side of my neck. His fingers flexed before he swung his gaze back to mine. "Who the hell are you?"

Smiling, I gently tapped his chest. "Riker Blackwood. A messed-up fox shifter who has two annoying brothers, a doting mother, and two pretty cool brother-in-laws. I'm also standing before a man I'd very much like to get to know because it's not every day a stranger kidnaps you to protect you."

With a snort, he shook his head. "It's crazy there's shifters."

That was what he latched onto?

Oh well.

"And vampires and fae."

He stilled.

Shit, it was probably wrong to say that and shock him more.

"But we can talk about that another night. Can I stay the night? In bed with you? We can cuddle or you could fuck my mouth—"

"Jesus, boy." His eyes darkened in a pissed way, not a good way. "You don't know me. Don't tell me you offer your body up to just anyone?"

His grip at my neck went to the front and tightened to drag me up into his body.

I thought he was trying to be intimidating, but honestly, I was just trying not to moan aloud. It probably wasn't the right moment.

Right?

"Tell me," he ordered, squeezing.

Screw it. The moan slipped free, and he froze. Only his eyes moved to run over my features. He probably saw the lust written clearly.

Would it be wrong to beg for him to grab me harder?

Probably.

"I don't offer to everybody. Haven't been with anyone in five years. What about you—No, don't answer that. It won't be good if you do."

His brows pinched again as his jaw clenched.

My poor guy is having a rough night.

I wondered if he still had his headache. I could offer to suck it out of him through his cock.

"Why wouldn't it be good?" he demanded, thumb sliding up and down on my skin.

Looking off to the side, I tried to stop the thought of my mate with someone else. It didn't help, though. Which was why my gaze narrowed when I stared back at him. I answered a little snappishly with the truth, "Because I'm a possessive shifter and if I *think* of you with someone else, I'll get *very* cranky. But if I *saw* you with someone else..." I laughed low, more sinister than humorous. "I *will* kill them. I'll slice at their throats, their stomachs, and hearts. I'll bath in their blood gleefully, knowing they'll never touch you again."

Panting, I closed my eyes and dropped my hands from him, stilling.

He'd stop touching me soon.

He'd seen what a freak I was. How hungry I could be for violence, and he'd run.

No, he'd kick me out and tell me he never wanted to see me again.

Invisible claws raked through my chest to dig into my heart.

His rejection would come.

A lead ball in my gut dropped to my feet.

I'd messed up already.

There wasn't a chance I could keep my cool, though. Not with *that* thought.

"I'm tired." His hand slipped from my throat.

I lifted my head so fast, I was surprised I didn't get whiplash.

"It's late. I need to go to bed," he added.

Oh.

Messaged received. He wanted me to leave. Bile, along with dread, rose. I swallowed it down.

Nodding, I took a step back, picked up my tee, and made it to the door.

There I heard, "Where the fuck're you goin'?"

Spinning back, I clasped my hands under my chin to try and hold my rapid heart inside my chest.

"You want to go to bed," I said.

"Yeah."

"Don't you want me to leave so you can do it?"

He shook his head and made his way to the hallway, dropping my wallet, which I'd forgotten, on the stand close by.

He wanted me to follow, right? I wanted to follow, so I was going to follow.

"I'll get the light," I called, plunging the room into darkness because the curtains were already drawn.

Then, in a thrilled skip, I went down the hall. It was his fault for not kicking me out when he had the chance after he'd discovered what a possessive fucker I was from what I'd said.

I stopped in the doorway he'd disappeared through. There were no curtains, so it left the moon to do the work of lighting the room. Not that it mattered if it was as dark as the living room. I'd be able to see him anyway.

Since I hadn't been far behind him, I didn't miss much. He'd already removed his vest and hung it over the arm of the chair in the corner. As he went back to the bed, which had to be a king size with how big it was, he took off his tee.

Biting down on my bottom lip, I pressed a hand to my belly as it tingled from the mouthwatering sight in front of me. The tattoos on his arm ended at his shoulder, and I couldn't see any more ink. What I did see was a hard, tanned, firm body with a dusting of chest hair. Enough I could rub against while I rode his cock.

He undid his jeans and pushed them down.

Boo.

His tight boxers stayed in place.

As soon as he'd kicked his jeans away, he climbed under the blankets and lay back with his hands behind his head while he watched me. I wanted to know what he was thinking. I wanted to pry his skull open to see how his brain ticked.

But I'd never hurt him.

Never. Not ever.

Thankfully, I hadn't put my tee back on. I just dropped it to the floor and went for my jeans, only to pause. "Is this an underwear sleepover or can I take them off?"

"On," he clipped.

Rolling my eyes, I smiled so he didn't think I was overly annoyed. If my mate wanted to get to know me before fucking my brains out, then I didn't mind at all.

The most special thing had already happened that night. Actually, there was more than one certain thing. There were a few things that showed me he was leaning toward wanting to keep me forever.

He'd saved me. Kidnapped me. Touched me. Wanted to fuck me. Was honest, and knew I was different, but he seemed to accept me the way I was. So far.

Nodding, I got rid of my jeans, then ran and jumped, landing on my hand and knees where I crawled up the mattress until I slumped down next to him under the blanket. I grinned at being beside my mate, happiness making my body hum.

I cocked a brow. "Sleep and no sexy time?"

His lips twitched, but he thinned them. Why did he keep stopping himself? "Sleep."

"Boo. But... can we cuddle a little at least?"

He sighed. "Fine."

"Yay!" I cried and scooted close. So close that my front was glued to his side, and I placed my arm over his wide chest, rubbing my cheek there. The hairs tickled. I liked it.

This was my favorite, forever man.

My fated mate.

I was so damn lucky. I hugged him tighter and mewed when he rested his arm along my back, hand to my waist.

Perfect.

CHAPTER THREE

CORBIN

Riker drifted off to sleep before I had last night. He was still asleep and curled into me with his arm and leg over me, holding tight. Like his limbs had been scared I'd leave in the middle of the night, so they'd latched on.

I couldn't leave, though.

I'd lain awake, asking myself what the fuck was I doing with this guy, but I couldn't come up with an answer.

Wrong.

All right, I did have an answer. It was simple really. The thought of not seeing Riker was like having an invisible hand wrap around my throat, choking me. It was why I hadn't kicked him out after his deadly confession.

The way he'd talked, the way his body had locked

down and his eyes had darkened when he told me he'd kill anyone who touched me, was clearly the truth.

He really would slaughter anyone who touched me.

I didn't know how I firmly knew, besides his body language hinting at it, but I did. And I always listened to my instincts since they'd gotten me out of situations before.

He was a tiny ball of viciousness.

I should be disgusted or annoyed by his intense obsession of me.

But I wasn't. And I didn't know if feeling satisfied over his possessiveness made me twisted, too, but I'd ended up grinning smugly over the thought of Riker cutting someone who'd screwed with me.

When he'd also told me that after I fucked him, I'd get to keep him forever, I was damn sure that was the truth too. At the time, I hadn't read into it, but fuck, I'd been up most of the night thinking and concluded that a lot of what he said had to be because he was a shifter.

I would be able to *keep* him if we fucked.

He *would* kill if he saw another flirt with me or if I was in trouble.

Holy fucking shit.

This tiny tornado was about to twist my world upside down, and I was ready for the ride.

Another thing I was slowly wrapping my head around was that there weren't only shifters, but vampires and fae as well.

I wasn't sure if I'd met or would meet any of them. Didn't bother me either way. My hands were already full of my little shifter anyway.

Christ, my brothers would think I'd hit my head and had lost my damn mind if I told them any of this.

I glanced down, and my heart skipped a beat seeing how peaceful he looked.

It was better than that other look he'd gotten in my living room. I had seen it when he'd been lost to his past. He'd seemed so broken for a few moments until there was a cheeky smirk on his face. But the broken part had already done its work by grabbing hold of me in a way that I wanted to do anything I could so he'd never have that look on his face again.

There was something about this boy that'd crawled under my skin and was now stuck.

Fuck.

It was his damn fault for saying shit about me fucking him and him protecting me that had called to another part of me that'd craved his actions. Now his fate was sealed to be stuck with me.

Christ, it sounded crazy even to me.

That I was ready to jump into something with a man because the thought of not seeing him was like a kick to the balls.

I'd try and take my time with him. Get to know him. But I only had so much strength, and if he kept offering himself to me, I was going to take him up on the offer.

I'd ruin him for everyone else so I could keep him forever.

Sighing, I ran my gaze over his hair and face. I was close to fearing my own thoughts. I'd become addicted to a person, a man who'd I'd known for less than a day and still barley knew anything about.

What I still wanted an answer to was why his brothers were looking to hurt him in the first place.

A smile tugged at my lips. If I had to guess, I suspected it was from something he'd done to them. I'd ask later.

Goddamn, I didn't want to look away from him. His head was tipped back as he snored softly, but there was another small noise too. Made me think of his fox.

A strand of his bright hair was close to falling over his eyes. I watched it in fascination as it slowly crept down and down. His nose scrunched up, cute as hell, when his hair tickled it.

I'd never watched anyone like this before. And hell, just the thought of looking away hurt my gut. I couldn't get enough. My past relationships or hookups had satisfied my baser instincts, but none had captured my attention like Riker did.

They didn't have me wanting to jump into something more like I did with him.

This really was something else, though.

What was growing, what connected us was different to anything I'd experienced. That Riker was a shifter was the only explanation. Not that I cared if there was some kind of magic at work to get me to notice him. I was hooked.

It didn't even matter what my brothers would say. They'd give me shit about falling hard for someone. It was what we did to each other. However, I also knew there were some assholes in the club who were bigoted. They'd never done or said anything in front of me, or I would've put a stop to it right then, but I'd heard a few brothers make a comment here or there about them.

Guess I'd see how they go when I took Riker in with me.

Although, that wasn't going to happen soon. I wanted him alone for a while.

First though, I needed coffee. I had a feeling I was going to need it to be on my toes when Riker woke up.

Slowly, I moved out from under him. He rolled away and shivered. I pulled the blanket over him and stood. Grabbing my jeans, I took them from the room to the bathroom. After taking a piss and washing my hands, I slipped them on.

Once in the kitchen, I yawned, scratched at my stomach, and hit the electric kettle. Fuck waiting for a coffee machine or water to boil on the stovetop. I needed that fix sooner. I grabbed two mugs and placed a teaspoon of instant coffee with two sugars in each.

As I waited for it to boil, I stretched and threw my arms up, cracking my back.

Fuck, that felt good.

Not as good as the arms winding around my waist.

"Mornin'," I said.

Riker hummed under his breath before inhaling loudly with his nose pressed to my skin between my shoulder blades.

Something wet ran over my skin.

"Did you just lick me?"

"Yep. You taste good." He moved around me, pushing in between the counter and my body. All he wore was his underwear, leaving his stunning body on display.

Fuck me, I wanted to sit him on the counter and just watch him like a creep.

With a grin, he said. "I had the best sleep being in bed with you. I'm going to have to stay again. Or you could come to my place. I'm sure my brothers want to meet you." He cocked his head to the side. "Though, they could show up here soon to check on me. Unless you want me to call them so they don't show up and we can have some morning sexy time?"

Snorting, I cupped his cheeks. "Call them. But we ain't jumpin' into the sack yet."

He beamed and wiggled in my hold. "You said *yet*."

Rolling my eyes, I pushed him out of the way and toward the phone on the wall. "Call. I'll make coffee. You want, yeah?"

"No, thanks. If I have coffee, I'm bouncing off the walls. One day Rio gave me an energy drink, and I had to run and run and run to get rid of some of the buzz." He jumped back at me, kissed my cheek, and skipped over to the phone.

Yeah, I had to remember to never give him coffee since it seemed all he needed to start the day was to wake up.

As soon as the kettle boiled, I poured the water into my mug, leaving enough room for creamer.

"Hey, bro ... Yes ... No ... I don't know ... Yes, he does. He's amazing and handsome and hot." He pouts. "No, we haven't. Even when I'd offered myself up, he didn't want to ... Yes ... Okay, I'll try and be patient ... You want to talk to him?" He thinned his lips and eyed me. "I don't think that's a good idea." I placed my coffee on the counter and stalked toward him, holding out my hand. Riker sighed. "He wants to talk to you too." When I was close, he hid the cordless phone behind his back. "Ignore anything he tells you about me. It's all lies. *Please* want me still after talking to him, and remember he has a bear inside him that makes him grumpy."

Please want me still.

A heaviness settled into my chest.

He was afraid of rejection.

From everyone or just me?

I threaded my fingers through the back of his hair and tugged him close, until the front of his body collided with mine. I kissed his forehead. "Nothin' he says will take away my interest in you."

He bit his bottom lip, smiled around it, and nodded.

"Pass me the phone, Riker," I ordered. When he did, I told him. "Go get a drink." I placed the receiver to my ear and watched him jog over to the refrigerator. His body was damn art. "Who's this?" I asked, even though I remember Riker saying it was Deacon who had the bear inside him.

"Deacon Blackwood. Riker's oldest brother, and you are Corbin James. President to the Fury MC. Only child. You live at—"

"Let's skip all the details I already know." A growl sounded through the phone. The bear was pissed. "You don't call me Corbin. Only Riker gets that. Name's Razor to you and the other brother. Respect me and I'll do the same in return. Now climb down off your high horse and tell me what you wanted?"

Riker cackled and danced from one foot to another while he drank some milk.

"Respect? Fine. In the most respectful manner, I'll warn you to be careful with our brother. Don't take him for granted. He's the type of person who gets attached to people, and they'll use that to their advantage. If I find out that is your end game, I'll make sure you pay. No matter who you are. No one fucks with Riker. Make sure you tread carefully, *Razor.*"

"Then I'll say back to you, *respectfully*, that you have nothin' to warn me against. So you can shove your threat up your bear's ass, and if you and the other one ever come at Riker like that again, I will fuckin' shoot you no matter what he's done."

There was nothing but silence for a few beats.

"Did he tell you what he did?"

"No. But for future reference, you come to me before dealing out any punishments. I can already read Riker, so I know he ain't no saint. He likes to play. But from now on, it'll be me deciding on his punishment or if he gets any at all. Hear me?"

A low chuckle. "Were you with men before, Riker?"

"No. Not that it's any of your business."

"Yet you're willing to take on Riker? Not only that but any situation he gets in, without considering what danger that could put on you? What about your club, Razor?"

"We can take care of ourselves. My brothers will have my back. If I protect Riker, they will too. If they don't have my back because of Riker in my life, then they'll have a choice of learning to accept or leave *my* club. Plus, you don't know what the brothers and I deal with. The danger we go through. Danger that won't touch Riker because I'd put a stop to it before anyone even fuckin' thought of harmin' him."

"Your club holds a bunch of vigilantes. You help clean the streets, which is why my brothers and I have left your club alone. Your club may grow and smoke your own pot, but it's nothing we're concerned about. I also know the club runs two gyms and five bars."

Tensing, I clipped, "How the fuck do you know this?" Who were these shifters?

"We have our resources. Don't fret, though. You'll know more about us soon. But the information you learn doesn't get shared with your club brothers because it could jeopardize Riker's life."

"I'd never fuckin' risk him."

I wouldn't. I never wanted to see him hurt in any way, but especially if I was the cause of it.

More damned silence from the other side.

I glanced up from the wooden planks on the floor to see that even Riker had stilled.

Running over what I'd said, I realized we hadn't even talked over what I'd already decided through the night. That I was ready to jump into this with him.

We *were* seeing where it went.

He wasn't backing out of something with me now.

"Ask Riker about fated mates" was all Deacon said before he ended the call.

Riker's gaze widened.

"You heard?" I asked, placing the phone back in its cradle.

His eyes darted all around me. He placed his glass down and started to back toward the hallway. "I have to go. I think. I don't know. But I'm suddenly worried."

"Why?"

Riker shook his head.

"If you move another step, I'll tan your ass, Riker Blackwood.'

He froze.

All except his lips, which tipped up into a wicked grin.

CHAPTER FOUR

RIKER

The fear over Corbin learning about fated mates and then rejecting the idea of being stuck with me forever fled when he decided to get kinky.

I placed my hands on my hips, grinned, and then said, "That's no punishment for me, big man. I like a bit of spanking. And choking. Hair pulling is a plus as well." I winked.

"Why were you worried?"

He popped my desire like a pin to a balloon. My shoulders sagged, and I dropped my hands. "No reason. But I would—"

"If you talk to me, I'll kiss you."

My cock perked up and decided it was time to fatten.

But is a kiss worth the risk of losing him when he hears about being mine?

Yes.

A kiss was worth the risk when the prize was my mate offering me those very kissable lips, which had more stubble surrounding them this morning. Would he grow a beard if I asked? I'd like to know what his beard would feel like between my legs while he ate my ass like it was the best treat in the world.

I'd never been with anyone who had a beard. But I could imagine Corbin with one. Dark like his hair. Black with maybe gray tinting it? Salt and pepper, then. I liked salt better than pepper because then I could call him my silver fox daddy.

A blast of arousal spread through my body, and I had to move from one foot to another, squeezing my ass cheeks together.

"Riker."

Right, kiss.

Yes, please.

Hopefully.

"I'm worried because I think that once you learn what a fated mate is you'll want me gone, and I'll never get to see you again." I waited for him to say something, but he didn't. My belly dropped, and I clutched my hands to my chest to push them against my rapid-beating heart. Reluctantly, I told him, "You and me, we're fated mates. There aren't many. Except for some reason, my brothers and I have been gifted with one. A fated mate forms a connection between us that lasts forever. It can't be broken and is sealed once we have sex and I bite you. I don't understand how it works, but it does, and it's something rare and wonderful. But the thought of you believing I'm not worth the trouble is like a sledge-hammer to the heart. I can be a handful, Corbin. I know it. My brothers know it. But I can't change who I am and what I do."

I was on a roll. Needing to tell him as much as I could.

"I took my brothers' partners to the club since I was bored and wanted a fight, and I knew my brothers would give me one when they got there. It was lucky Soren, the club owner who is a vampire and loves me, got everyone out before the hurt went down. But then you kidnapped me...." A huff of air spilled out of me before I dragged in another deep breath.

I shook my head and hugged myself, rocking forward and back on my feet. "I'm getting off track. I do stupid stuff like that all the time when I'm bored—not getting off track, I mean like at the nightclub—and it can bring a world of danger into my life and in return your life, but that's if...." I shook my head again.

Should I carry on? It's not like he's running for the door yet.

Fuck it.

"My job is dangerous too. We don't only work in the family businesses, which can be so freaking boring as well, but my brothers and I work for our shifter council in elim-inating anyone they tell us to. Bad people. But we don't kill just those they tell us. We'll slaughter anyone who does us wrong or tries to hurt us or anyone we love."

By the time I was done—at least I thought I was done, but I wasn't too sure—I was panting.

I looked off to the side but peeked at my mate out the corner of my eye.

He rolled his head around, and I heard a crack in his neck. "Who's this vampire that you were talkin' about?"

I jolted in shock and stared at him. "Huh?"

"The vampire that loves you."

My heart danced up into my throat, but I swallowed it back down. "Are... are you jealous?"

Oh my God, that was the cutest thing ever. No one ever got jealous over me. No one cared enough to get jealous. Then again, I hadn't liked anyone enough to want them around long enough to get jealous. It was possible that if they'd gotten jealous, I would have punched them.

But with Corbin—my sweet, angry angel—I loved that he got jealous.

"Was he that guy with long hair standing at the bar?" he asked roughly.

I couldn't tell him. I didn't want him to get hurt. Not that I thought Soren would, but there was a chance Soren would drink from him, and if that happened, if Soren touched my mate, I would kill him, and that'd make me upset. Even my belly revolted at the thought of Corbin being touched and me killing Soren.

So, instead of answering him, I asked, "Aren't you scared about being a fated mate?"

"No."

My insides danced in glee like my fox was.

"Why?"

Stop questioning him, you fool. He'll run for sure if I keep checking if he's certain about me and us and our future.

"Decided last night that I wanted to see where this was going with us. Being a fated mate explains why I already feel so strongly, and it sounds a lot like marriage without divorce. I reckon I'll take you up on the offer of keepin' you forever since I already don't like the thought of not seein' you. But it ain't like we gotta rush this and bond right now. I don't want you to think I'd be accepting you just to fuck you." Corbin took a step closer, and I vibrated with need, even just to touch him. "As soon as I saw you, Riker, I knew there was somethin' different and special about you. I won't want to change who you are. But I'd try and advise you if I think somethin' you're doin' is a risk to you or me."

He stopped close, but not close enough that I could reach out and lay my hands on him. Hands that itched to have our mate's skin under them.

I wanted to rub my face against his warmth too. Not only in my fox form, but as I stood now. We wanted him stinking of our scent.

I won't want to change who you are.

He'd said it and I believed him.

"Come here, Riker," he clipped.

I bounced, ran the few steps, and jumped into his arms. He caught me with ease, one arm under my ass, the other at the back of my head to pull me into him for that much-needed kiss.

I moaned into his mouth and parted my lips after the first touch. I needed his taste to mingle with mine, and holy guacamole, he tasted fine.

He groaned into my mouth when I scraped my nails over his shoulders. He threaded his fingers through my hair and tightened. A sharp sting had me grinding into him and nipping at his bottom lip.

He tried to pull back, but I followed, assaulting him with more kisses.

Until his hand switched to grab the front of my neck and squeeze.

"Enough," he ordered. "Enough for now. Be a good boy and I'll give you my mouth later."

I whimpered, dazed with desire. I rolled my cock into his lower stomach. "Can I touch you, please? Can I suck you? Need your cock in my mouth. Want your cum down my throat—"

When he choked me harder, I groaned and gasped, eyes rolling back.

He placed me on my feet and forced me to kneel on the floor.

Yes, yes, yes, yes.

Saliva pooled in my mouth when he released his hold around my throat and ran his hand to the side of my face to stick his thumb in my mouth. I sucked greedily and squeezed my own cock to starve off the orgasm tickling at the edge already.

With his other hand, he undid the zipper of his black jeans, and I whimpered.

Reaching in, he pulled his cock out. Long, thick, and veiny, just the way I liked it. I already knew my ass would be sore from taking him, and I couldn't wait for the hard fucking I knew he'd deliver.

I couldn't wait for the bond either.

"Is this what you want?"

Humming, I nodded, and he withdrew his thumb. "Yes, Sir. Please." A tingle raced up my spine when Corbin's eyes heated over the word "sir." I'd scented his arousal the first time I used it and knew I'd want to again. The heady rush of desire knowing it pleased him was addicting.

I shuffled close on my knees and stuck my nose into his skin at the side of his dick, drawing in a deep breath.

My cock leaked in my underwear. I had to pull it free to stroke over it.

Fingers glided into my hair and tightened, tugging my head back.

"Hand off your cock, boy."

Noooo. I pouted, but he stared down at me with a smirk that didn't match his darkened eyes.

His grip tightened more, causing another sting to my scalp.

I scrapped my top teeth over my bottom lip.

"Christ, you really do love this." On *this*, he pulled at my hair again.

"Yes," I moaned, hand slowly sliding across my stomach and down to—

"If you touch yourself, you don't get my cock."

When I glared up at him, he chuckled.

I stuck my tongue out and waited for my prize since I was going to be a good fox to get what I wanted.

He took hold of his cock and tapped his wet tip to my tongue. "Fuck," he clipped. "Close your lips around it."

I did and he thrust into my mouth, hit the back of my throat, and I choked, eyes watering.

He went to pull away, but I gripped the back of his thighs to hold him in place while I opened my throat more and swallowed around him.

Snot, saliva, and tears soaked my face.

Corbin cursed up a storm and tore me off his cock using my hair. I was about to pout and beg, but he thrust in again. Right to the back, and I moaned, my own dick jerking up and down as cum shot out, landing on the floor.

"Christ, boy," Corbin snarled. He pulled out and thrust in again. My throat warmed from his load spraying down it. He groaned and grunted through his release as I swallowed each drop.

I lost his cock but was picked up and carried to the counter where my mate kissed me.

He didn't care I was a mess. He claimed my mouth like he couldn't get enough.

He drew away and rested his forehead to mine. We both fought for our breaths.

"Haven't come that fast in decades."

Cackling, I squeezed my legs around his waist, my spent cock rubbing against him. "Me neither. But I liked it. A lot. It was damn hot, and I can't wait to do it again. I'll suck your cock anytime, anywhere. I don't even care if we're down the street and you want my mouth. You can have it. I'll drop to my knees as soon as you demand it, Sir."

"Hell, Riker."

This feeling, this lightness was like when I hunted. When I killed. And I wanted it all the time.

Corbin said he accepted me, he'd take me as I was, and he would soon tie his life with mine.

I... I couldn't understand how a person could make another giddy, but there I was, feeling it in that moment, and now I knew how lucky I was. Maybe after everything I'd done, I wasn't as condemned as I thought I was.

Why else would Fate give me someone who balanced me out perfectly?

I deserved this.

Him.

And I'd take him.

He really didn't know what he was getting into. How cold I could be. How ruthless, and hard, and possessive— so *very* possessive. He may have had a small glimpse of what I was like, but not all. So, I'd have to get him addicted to me before he could run away.

He was mine to keep. Like I was his.

There was no escape now that I'd had his cock in my mouth and his cum down my throat.

CHAPTER FIVE

CORBIN

Later that afternoon, we sat on the couch watching an action movie from one of the apps, when Riker asked me his sixteenth question.

"Favorite sex position?"

Smirking, I shook my head slightly. When he'd asked to play twenty questions, I'd said no to begin with. Until he begged and gave me those damn puppy-dog eyes. But hell, I found myself actually enjoying this shit.

"Doggie style. You?"

He groaned and slapped my chest. "You can't keep asking me the same questions. But, since this is about sex, I'll answer. I'm a missionary kind of shifter. I like it sweet, but steamy. Rough and hot. Well, any way you want to give it."

"I'd thought my brothers were horny fuckers, but you're taking the cake."

He moaned. "I love cake." That wasn't the only thing I'd learned about him either. He preferred a meat lover's pizza over hamburgers. He wished he could sit still enough to read a romance book because he heard the ones about shifters were hotter than hell. He enjoyed annoying his brothers. He wanted to go to a live concert one time. He hated the library because he got shushed all the time.

The more he shared, the more I wanted to know.

"What's your—" My phone on the coffee table rang. I scowled at it, hating we were interrupted even when we weren't doing much.

"Boo," Riker complained when I nudged him away from lounging on me as I leaned forward to grab the device.

Snorting, I told him, "You could have moved yourself."

"Nope." He snuggled in when I rested back.

This was the most I'd seen him settled without twitching. I didn't know if it was that the movie and our conversation that was entertaining enough for him to sit still or if it was because he got to stick close to me.

Either way, I liked it. But I also enjoyed his bounce-off-the-walls energy.

After curling my arm around him, I answered the call to my closest friend, who was also the vice president to the club. "Spade." The noise in the background told me he was either at one of our bars or the compound.

He said something, but I wasn't listening. Instead, my

attention latched onto Riker's smooth legs that were thrown over one of mine.

A deep craving to have them wrapped around my waist while he rode me grew.

This connection was a goddamn rush.

I didn't know if I would've ever noticed another guy, but it wasn't something I needed to think about. The man I now had in my life was all that mattered.

"You listenin' to me?" Spade asked.

"No," I told him, tracing a hand up and down Riker's thigh and underwear-covered ass.

Spade chuckled. "You could'a just told me you were busy with a woman."

Riker stilled and a growl started to form from him.

Shit.

"No woman," I told Spade. "What do you want?"

"I said I finally got through to Pauly about our missin' order from Harley's yesterday. Pauly's sayin' the bill hasn't been paid."

What the fuck?

Pauly was our booze supplier. He gave it to us at a discounted price because we helped him out with some hooch for his family. So why hadn't the invoice been paid when I knew we weren't hard-up and could pay the damn bill?

"I'm presumin' you checked in with our money man?" I asked.

Writer was our treasurer; he took care of the money in the club. I'd known him since I prospected in. He'd already been a brother and appointed that position. He never steered us wrong before.

Spade sighed. "You might want to come into the compound for this."

Fuck.

"You can't deal with it?"

"Brother, I had Monkey look into a couple of things. Some of it's dodgy."

Riker shifted off me as I sat forward. "What the fuck you mean?"

"Better I show you."

Sighing, I scrubbed a hand over my face. I did not need this.

"Fuckin' hell, Spade. Fine. I'll be there in ten."

"Catch'a."

Grunting, I hung up and scrubbed a hand over my face. Why the hell would Writer do this shit in the first place, but more so why now?

Looking left, I said, "Have to head to the club, Riker."

He pulled his legs up to kneel on the couch. "Okay." His lips thinned, and I knew it was to stop himself from saying more again. His arms wrapped around his waist, as if he was holding himself still.

Christ. I wanted to take him with me, but I also didn't.

We'd only had one night and half a day together. I shouldn't have been so attached already.

Yet, I was, and I knew this between us was for the long haul. I wanted him like he did me, and what we already had was bigger than any human partnering.

Fate had picked us for one another, and that cosmic shit was intense.

They couldn't be wrong. I'd trust their choice. It was easy to since I was already obsessed.

Reaching over, I picked him up with ease to pull him onto my lap. His knees slid to my hips, his hands on my chest.

I squeezed his waist gently. "Talk to me, sunshine."

Before he dropped his face into my chest, I caught his smile from me calling him sunshine. I thought the name was damn perfect for him because he was a big ray of sunshine that had warmed me and my life more than it'd ever been.

Against my chest, he muttered, "Just feeling funny about you going."

"Know what you mean. Which is why you're comin'."

He gasped, sitting up. "Really?"

I smirked. "Yeah."

Fuck it. The brothers would meet him sooner than I anticipated, but I didn't care.

"Are you sure? These are your people, your club. You've never been with a guy before around them or at all, right?"

I shook my head.

"What will they think? They could be mean to you about it, and I'd hate to have to kill anyone you like. You'd tell me if you like them enough to keep them alive, yeah? I mean, I'll try not to kill anyone, but if I can tell you're pissed about something they say, you might have to hold me back.... Maybe it's best I stay here."

Christ, he was fucking cute. I probably shouldn't find his murderous tendencies adorable, but I did.

"I ain't leavin' you here, sunshine. Need you with me."

His body jolted, and his smile grew slower, but bigger than I'd seen. "Okay." He popped up off me and ran from the room.

"Where are you goin'?"

"To get dressed and grab some knives. I left mine at home."

Shit.

"Riker, leave the knives," I called, standing, and making my way over to pick up my keys. I slipped on my boots and my cut as I listened to him rushing back.

"Boo, my boo, really?" he asked.

Did he just call me boo?

I wasn't sure if I liked it or not, but I wasn't touching it for now.

"Yes." I dipped in and kissed him swiftly. Knew if I lingered, we wouldn't get out the door. He was back, dressed in the clothes from the night before. We'd have to stop at his place and grab some more. "Get your shoes on. You need a jacket?"

He bounced back and forth on his feet with his hands clasped together in front of him. "I'm good. Shifters always run hotter than humans."

Nodding, I went out the door and locked it after we were out. I would have enjoyed taking my ride, with Riker warming my back, but I didn't have a spare helmet yet. We headed to my car instead.

I'd always refused to take anyone on my bike until I knew that person would be important in my life.

Looked like I needed that helmet now.

Christ. I smiled to myself at how I was already including Riker in things.

I didn't do shit by halves. I went all in. But at least I was sure about this with him.

"Do you ride?" I asked when he got into the passenger seat.

"I could ride you," he offered sweetly, almost coyly, but I knew there was a devil underneath all that, and I fucking loved it.

Lips twitching, I started the car and reversed out, saying, "Another time." Once driving, I asked again, "Motorbikes, Riker. Have you ridden one before?"

"I have two. A Harley and a Buell 1125R. I like speed, but I like to cruise too. Can we go for a ride one day? I'll try and slow down for you." He grinned.

Snorting, I reached over and took his hand in mine, resting them on my thigh. "I'd like that."

When I glanced at him, since he was quiet and still, I saw the softness in his gaze as he stared down at our joined hands.

He enjoyed my attention on him. Didn't matter being with a guy was new for me. I wanted to touch him, so I did it. Besides, some of those soft emotions expanded my chest from knowing he liked the attention.

"This feels natural," I told him.

His head popped up, gaze locked onto mine, lips smiling. "It does and I love it. I like that you know everything there is and still want me around. It makes me so happy that you already know about my animal. My belly won't stop fluttering." He bounced in the seat a bit and cackled.

"Bet that was a surprise. Seeing Deacon and then hearing I'm one too."

"The biggest." I nodded.

"And you're handling it so well. Way better than Rio and Kieran. I should give you head again for it."

Chuckling, I shook my head. "Later. Let's deal with this shit, go get dinner someplace, grab some more clothes for you, and head back to mine."

"Then?"

"Then you can tell me how *you* like your dick sucked."

He gasped and pulled our hands up to hold them against his chest. "Really?"

"Yeah, sunshine."

"Yay!" he cheered and palmed his hardness while mine twitched under my jeans.

"For now, tell me who Rio and Kieran are."

"They're the best. Not as good as you. No one will ever be as good as you. Rio is Deacon's fated, and Kieran is Nox's. Deacon found Rio first. We killed his father because he was dealing drugs and other stuff to the public."

Holy shit. He just blurted that out. Obviously, his trust of me formed from being his fated. Satisfaction had me smiling, knowing I got to be privy to all the details.

"Then Nox stalked Kieran, who was Rio's professor when Rio went to college. Then Kieran got mugged. Nox saved him and killed his muggers. Now they're joined at the hip ever since." He nipped at my fingers and grinned. "Kinda like you and me."

I winked over at him. "Couldn't resist gettin' you outta there."

53

We stopped outside the gates to the compound. I flicked a couple of fingers to the brothers on guard and waited for them to open the electric gates.

Riker peered out the window with what looked like awe since his mouth hung open.

I'd like to know what he saw. To me, the space out front left for bikes and cars was a boring gravel area. The building was an old hotel that Pops had bought back in the day, and we really hadn't done much to it. It held a large conference room where we met for church. A dining room that we used for our common area since it was off the kitchen. We hadn't needed all the table and chairs, so they were to the left of the room and the right was where we added in some couches, billiards tables, and a bar. There were three offices, two were for Coms, our tech brother. The last was my own, and then thirty bedrooms all with their own bathroom.

"This place is big. I think it's bigger than our house. Maybe older, but way cool."

Grunting, I pulled to a stop and got out of the car. Riker was quick to get to my side, looking all around us. With my palm to his lower back, I guided him inside and down the hall toward the common room where Spade'd be waiting. I could already hear the low bass of the music so no doubt Riker would too.

It was then I realized things could go wrong.

I didn't have to worry about the old ladies. None of them would make a move on Riker or, more importantly, me in front of Riker.

How-fucking-ever, we had women here that we called club bunnies. They only dropped by to party and fuck.

They liked trying to get into my bed since I was the president. A lot of them hoped they'd be the one to tie me down so I'd put a ring on their finger.

They were about to learn things had changed and they wouldn't be happy.

We had some good ones, sweet ones even. But there were a couple of real bitches who tried to lord over all the other women there. Those types were never something I was into.

I'd preferred the sweet and good ones.

And yet, I had my own type of wild and sweet now.

Guess I'd soon see how things would go down. I always liked a challenge anyway.

CHAPTER SIX

RIKER

Corbin opened the door where the party was happening. There were about thirty people hanging about. Men and women of all types. Some were chilling and chatting while drinking. Others played billiards and smoked. And then there were the men fucking women out in the open. They also weren't picky about which hole they took. There were only a few, but enough that was distracting.

Which was why I didn't see the woman getting close until she was at Corbin's other side.

For a quick moment, he stopped and stilled when she curled her hands around his upper arm.

But what shot a rush of giddiness into my body was when he shook her off.

I wanted to pat his cock and tell her *mine* and then

praise him for brushing off her touch by dropping to my knees and sucking him off again.

Maybe I should breathe in her face and ask her if she could smell his cum.

"Razor." She pouted up at him.

Only I could pout at Corbin.

Dancing around his back, I slipped in between him and her.

Her gaze flicked over me and swept up to Razor with a sneer. "Who the fuck is this?"

"Who the fuck are you?" I asked, and since her attention didn't even come back to me, I took a step closer. When it snapped down on me, I smiled, running my tongue over my top teeth. She was taller than me. Some might say prettier. She was also the type who thought her position was at the top among the men. It was easily read in the way she held herself.

Where were my knives when I needed them? Oh, right. Not here. I wanted to slice off her hands for touching him. What would also be fun was if I could shove a grenade in her mouth and watch her head explode for even looking at *my* mate with lust.

Walking around her, I offered, "From now on, you'll want to rethink when it comes to the president. He's not to be touched, and no one even *thinks* they can sleep with him. You may talk to him, but from far away. Do you understand me?"

She laughed, but it was tight with tension. Good. I had her full attention as she watched me circle around and around her.

"You've got to be joking."

At least, as I sized up my prey, I noticed we hadn't caught everyone's attention. Only some. Though, the women who were looking weren't coming to the aid of their friend. Or maybe this piece didn't have any friends. I wouldn't be surprised.

"I'm not joking, doll." I stopped just behind her and whispered into her ear, "This will be your only warning. You don't know me, so you shouldn't even try guessing if you can take me on or have Razor take your side. He won't. He's mine now, and if I even smell you close to him, I will cut your pretty little head off." A low growl rolled out of me.

She'd tensed, and the amazing aroma of fear wafted off her.

An arm slid around my waist, and I was lifted off my feet as Corbin carried me over to the bar, sitting me on a stool.

I looked up at him and grinned when I didn't see any anger or worry coming from him. "At least I didn't cut off her hands for touching you."

His lips twitched. "That's only because I didn't let you bring knives."

My grin grew. "You know me so well already." I hugged him to me, pressing my face into his chest.

Whispers started as the music was turned down. My mate wouldn't hear the chatter. Only I could with my shifter senses.

"Who's that with the prez?"

"Why is Razor lettin' some guy hug him?"

"What's goin' on?"

"That shit is sick."

"I knew that fucker was gonna run this club to the ground."

That one I didn't like. That one I would remember and make note of the voice. If I heard it again or saw the man, I would point him out to Corbin in case he was trouble later for him. Me, I didn't care what anyone thought. If my mate was happy, I would be too. But if some murdering got thrown in with that happiness, I'd be an ecstatic little fox.

"Are you seriously going to let him talk to me like that?"

I rolled my forehead on Corbin's chest to the side and stared at the same female who was close to signing her own death.

She saw me peeking just as I imagined the blood running from her neck after I sawed it open. Maybe she could read my mind because she took a step back. I smiled.

"Harper, you need to heed Riker's warning," Corbin told her. "Let it be known to the other girls too."

She snorted. "You've got to be fucking kidding me. What is this?"

I dropped my hands, my head, and breathed.

Kill.

Kill.

Kill.

The thought drilled into me over and over. I wanted to claw out her eyes. Cut off her tongue and gut her. Even my fox desired to devour her innards for talking to our mate like that.

My body vibrated with the hunger for her blood.

Slowly, I lifted my head enough to look out and lock on my prey.

Another growl sounded from my chest. One I couldn't stop.

Anger burned under my skin. I scraped my fingers up and down my thighs to try and stop the need to attack.

Corbin stepped in front of my view.

"Fuck off, Harper. Now."

"But—"

"Bitch, you heard the prez. Get the fuck away," a hard voice said off to our side.

With a huff, Harper scattered.

Corbin faced me.

"Riker?"

My upper lip trembled as I kept my snarl at bay. I didn't want to hurt or be mean to my mate because I couldn't control my hunger for her blood.

A gasp suddenly escaped me when my head was yanked back by my hair.

Corbin's concerned gaze studied me.

He pinched my cheeks in his other hand. "Focus on me."

He yanked again, and the second sting had me smiling. "Let's hope she listened," I said.

"I'll make sure of it."

"Or you could just manhandle me like this into listening to you." I threw in a wink to let him know I'd reined in the hunt.

His smirk told me he knew.

But he didn't understand what a momentous moment that was. It'd always been hard for me to stop and lock down the need. Yet, he'd controlled my body and mind in a way that it took seconds to switch me up and calm me down.

He really was my perfect mate.

"I'll make sure to remember that," Corbin said with humor in his gaze.

I loved him already.

I really did.

It shone out of me, and I was surprised he didn't see it.

Or maybe he could when his expressions softened, warmed.

"Someone gonna introduce me?"

Corbin leaned in. My heart hammered inside my chest.

Was he really going to claim me in front of his family just like this?

Hope blossomed, and I wanted to palm my hard dick.

When his lips touched mine, I opened up to him and he took it. His tongue fought with mine. Teeth nipped. Lips sucked.

Whispered words swept through my superior hearing.

"Holy shit."

"Is he serious?"

"That's fuckin' disgustin'."

Their words weren't an issue. I didn't care what anyone thought.

I only cared for Corbin. Only my mate.

But I'd find who'd said those things and watch them. Wait for when they stepped out of line to deal with them.

With Corbin's hand around the front of my neck, he pushed me away from the kiss, then released his hold on me before he straightened and stepped to my side to stare at his men. His brothers.

No one moved and Corbin said nothing. He just waited to see if they had anything to say about his decision, and honestly, it was the hottest thing I'd seen in a long time.

He commanded the room with a look, with a raised brow, and no one questioned their leader of his choice in me.

Beautiful.

I couldn't wait to tell my brothers what a badass my mate was. Not that their mates weren't great. They were. Mine was just better.

As I looked around, I couldn't contain my glee. I bounced up to stand on the stool and then jumped to Corbin's back. He caught me with ease because he was *badass.*

The man closest to us snorted and chuckled. I glanced to him and saw his grin. He seemed around the same age as Corbin, so I presumed he was Spade. He was good-looking, just not as handsome as Corbin.

"Now that's outta the way. You gonna tell me who he is?" Corbin's friend, who looked like a buff, tattooed Viking with dark blond hair and light brown eyes, asked.

When Corbin turned, I slipped down off him as the people went back to what they were doing beforehand. Except the ones fucking. That mood got killed. I didn't understand why. I was hornier now after seeing my mate being the boss.

Corbin took the stool I'd been on and sat. He pulled me between his legs and wrapped his arms around me.

I bounced within his hold, grinning wildly.

"Spade, Riker. Riker, Spade. My vice president and friend."

"Hey, Spade. I'm guessing that's your club's name. What's your real name?"

Spade chuckled and shook his head as Corbin tightened his hold around me. "Nah, sunshine. You don't get his Christian name. We only share them with our significant others."

"Is that why I get to call you Corbin, but my brothers will have to use Razor?"

Something shattered on the concrete floor.

We glanced over to see a blushing woman who had accidently tipped her tray. Smugly, I knew the slip-up was over me calling Corbin by his name, which told her that I really was important to him.

I loved that. And him. I so very much loved him with every part of mine and my fox's body. We wanted to claim him. We wanted him fucking us and coming in our ass while I bit him to complete the bond.

Then he'd be mine forever.

Well, not forever, but a very long time, and anyone who tried to hurt him, I would hunt and kill.

"Yeah, sunshine," Corbin said in my ear.

Oh, right. The name conversation. I tipped my head to the side, and he brushed his lips over my cheek. I hummed, and said, "I really want to climb you like a tree and have you fuck me so hard that I can't walk for days."

"Fuck," my mate clipped.

"Hot damn," Spade said with a grin.

Cackling, I turned in Corbin's embrace and kissed his

jaw. "It'll have to wait. I'm gonna go make nice with the women and politely warn them away from you."

"Riker," he warned.

"I said *politely*."

"Call me over if anyone says shit before you start killin', yeah?"

Spade snorted. He didn't believe my mate, but at least Corbin knew me. I patted his chest, wanting to purr.

A heady rush of warmth had me beaming up at him. I saluted. "You got it, Sir."

I went over to the woman who'd dropped the bottles. Someone had already swept the mess up, so I helped by taking the tray off her.

"These for your friends?" I nodded toward the group of women sitting in the couch area. A couple of others were scattered about flirting with the men, but I wanted to meet the main group where Harper had come from. It was lucky, for her sake, that she was no longer in the room.

"Y-Yes," she answered.

"I've got them," I told her, and used my other hand to wave her on.

I glanced back and saw Corbin watching me. I winked. He smirked. I could still feel his eyes on me when I followed Clumsy.

"So?" I heard Spade ask my mate. "How long you known the kid?"

Corbin chuckled. "Would you believe he's thirty-six?"

"Fuck off."

"Saw his ID myself and known him a little while."

"Razor—"

"Save it. I know what I'm doin'. He's something else,

something special, and I don't want to imagine a day without him in it."

"Jesus. He put a spell on you?"

He huffed. "Yeah, somethin' like that. You'll like him when you get to know him."

"Yeah but...."

"What?"

"Brother, I saw the look in his eyes when Harper was over here gettin' in your face. It was why I helped send her on her way. He definitely seemed like he was contemplating murder."

"He probably was. But he won't because he knows he needs my permission to end anyone in my life first."

"Fuck me, Razor. You gone and lost your mind? Was your warning an actual warning to not kill anyone?"

"Yeah." He chuckled like he liked my monster side. *Yippee.* "But he and his brothers are like us. We protect those who are important to us by any way possible. Even if it means we get our hands dirty. Riker's just a little more protective and possessive of me, is all."

Oh my God, he sounded positively proud about me being that way.

Which was why it was easy to fall for my mate.

Taking my attention from their conversation, I stopped in front of the group and beside the clumsy girl. Smiling, I placed the tray on the table and straightened.

"Hello, it's a pleasure to meet you all." I grinned, tucking my hands into the pockets of my jeans as I rolled from heel to toes. "My name's Riker, and I belong to Razor, who I call Corbin."

Lips parted. Gasps sounded. Eyes widened.

They got it.

"I would very much appreciate that none of you lay a hand on him or talk to him in a flirty way, so I don't have to...." I stilled and wiped my smile away as I tried to think of the best way of saying I would hunt and kill them. "Express my displeasure upon your body in a very unpleasant way."

They all stared for a few moments. Most looked well warned because I could scent their fear. All except one.

A woman with long brown hair and gorgeous unmarked skin hooted out a laugh. "I like you. Displeasure upon your body. You're hilarious."

"And serious," I told her.

"Oh, I know." She nodded and stood. She was almost my height but just that touch smaller, which made her adorable. She grabbed one of the drinks. "All the ladies about peed themselves. Which is why you don't have to worry about us coming near the president now that you've claimed him." After a sip, she added, "My name's Lynnette." She went on to introduce the others, and I tried to take in all their names, but the only one I remembered was the first. Oh, besides Clumsy, who was Darlene.

"Hi to all." I smiled. "Are any of you friends with that Harper lady?"

"She thinks she has friends, but most of them only play nice with her because she'll cut someone if she thinks we're stabbing her in the back," Lynnette explained.

"Except you, Lynnette," Darlene whispered.

I patted the shy Darlene on the head, even though I had to reach up a little.

Lynnette snorted. "I know I have a knife coming my

way any day, but I've just been lucky that I'm not going after any of the men she wants to try and become an old lady to."

"An old lady?" I asked. The others started to relax and grab a drink for themselves from the tray I set down.

"That's when the men in the club claim their wife, or partner, in your case."

My nose screwed up. "I'm an old lady?" I didn't like that title.

Some of the women laughed, but it was Lynnette who said, "Honey, you can be called whatever you want."

"I'm Corbin's man. His man." I nodded. "Wait, I should call him Razor around people, right?"

"Damn, Riker, you really are his man. Good for you claiming the most wanted guy in the club, and you call him whatever you want. We'll still respect him by using his club name."

"Thank you." I grinned. "And since he's mine, I'm a part of the club now. So, I think that if any of you have a problem with say, Harper, you come to me, and I will gladly deal with her or anyone else who'll try to fuck you over."

She patted my arm. "Aren't you the sweetest."

"I can be," I said with a smile and then I lost it when I added, "But then I'm also not if anyone messes with me or mine." With my smile back in place, since I liked these women so far, I took Darlene's hand and moved us over to a free couch, pulling her down with me. I patted the other free spot next to me for Lynnette to sit. "Come, come. Tell me what I need to know so I'm the best man for my man."

She grinned. "You're going to be good for this club, Riker. I believe it."

I wanted to be good. But I also liked to be mean. They would only see that side if or when someone screwed with Corbin.

CHAPTER SEVEN

CORBIN

I couldn't stop looking at Riker. He confidently walked up to the group of women, said something that had a few losing color, but they seemed to calm once he and Lynnette started talking. Immediately after, he was sitting and laughing with them. Like he'd known them a lot longer than a few minutes.

"You really are smitten with him," Spade commented.

I grunted. Riker threw his head back and cackled as he patted Lynnette on the head, like he had Darlene just before.

He was gorgeous.

"You think you can tear your eyes away from him for a moment while we go to your office and talk?"

Christ. I didn't want to, but I had to.

"Let me tell him, and I'll meet you there."

Spade chuckled and slapped me on the back. "This shit is good to see, brother."

Smiling, I handed him the keys and tipped my chin up at him before I made my way over to the group. They quieted when I got close.

"Riker, gonna hit the office for a bit. You good here or wanna come back?"

The women looked from me to him. He beamed. "You go do your business, boss man, and come back to me when you can."

I raised a brow.

"Promise I'll be good."

"We'll only get him up dancing with us—"

"Like fuck," I clipped at Lynnette.

She laughed. "Jealousy suits you, Razor."

Rolling my eyes, I locked them back on Riker. "Back soon."

He blew me a kiss, which had my lips twitching. I shook my head and stalked off to the back rooms where my office was.

Spade sat opposite my desk, waiting. I walked around and rested my ass down. "What you were hintin' at over the phone is that you think Writer's messin' with our books?"

Spade nodded.

"When I walked in, I saw Writer's in for a good night." He'd been out there drinking while playing pool as Shirley rubbed herself up against him. "And when he saw me come in, he tensed, until Shirley drew his attention away. You think he suspects we're catchin' on?"

"Maybe."

"How much he taken?"

Spade thinned his lips and pulled a notebook out. My gut soured. I knew from his troubled expression, I wouldn't like his answer. "About fifteen thousand. But that's only going back as far as this year." He pushed the notebook my way, and I took a look.

Fucking hell. What a cunning motherfucker.

"Does he know you contacted Pauly about the order?"

He snorted. "Funny thing. Pauly rang me just before you rocked up. The bill just got paid. Writer ducked off to piss before, and he must have been notified of the fuck up. If Pauly hadn't called, we wouldn't have looked at his books in the first place."

Exactly.

Writer was the one who divided up the monthly profit our businesses made and paid into our accounts. The higher the placement in the club, the higher the amount we got. I never questioned mine because I was sitting pretty with what was in my bank account.

"Well, let's leave Writer thinkin' he got away with this while we have Coms set up surveillance—in our own fuckin' club—for Writer's rooms. I want hard proof in case he tries to talk his way outta this with some bullshit we haven't thought about. But we also need to make sure he's actin' on his own in this shit. We'll reconvene in a couple'a days. Get Shirley to drug the fucker so he goes down hard tonight. I want the cameras set up by mornin'."

Spade grinned. "You got it, Prez. Want to see more of his books?"

"Nah, brother. From what you've shown, I trust you

and Monkey aren't talkin' out your asses about this. Thank fuck you guys found this." Spade, Monkey, Coms, and a few others were the brothers who had my complete trust.

"So, you know why I got you in here, yeah?"

Smirking, I nodded. "Known you a long time, brother. You needed me to approve the shit you'd already considered doin' but didn't want to give too much away over the phone."

"Damn right. The only difference was that I'd thought about gettin' Writer outta the way with a ride, but he might not take to that if he's havin' fun. Gettin' Shirley to drug him will be easier to keep an eye on him."

"Not just a pretty face, Spade."

He snorted. "You don't do it for me, brother."

Someone banged on the door.

"Enter," I barked.

Monkey stuck his head through with a grin. "Your guy just handed Roadie his ass for touchin' one of the girls who didn't want his attention for the night."

Shit.

I was up out of my chair and down the hall in moments with my brothers following. The crowd parted, and I spotted Riker kneeling on my brother's spine with Roadie's arm pinned behind his back. He whispered something in his ear, and I saw my brother's face screwed up in pain, but it was also pale with fear.

Riker glanced up and his words stopped. My sunshine jumped up to stand with his hands clasped behind his back. "I didn't kill him," he announced, and some of the crowd laughed. They thought he was joking. That he wouldn't kill. They didn't see what I saw lingering underneath.

"Come here," I demanded. Riker skipped over while Roadie stayed on the floor.

Riker placed his hands on my waist and looked up. "He just walked up to Darlene and grabbed her boobie. I could tell she didn't want his hands on her like that. Hasn't he ever heard of foreplay?"

Fuck me, I wanted to laugh. *Grabbed her boobie.*

Instead, I rubbed a hand over my mouth and curled him into me. Together, we stared down at Roadie. "What did you do to him?"

"Pfft, nothing much. He's overacting. Get up, Roadie," Riker called, and my brother slowly got to his feet.

"Nothin' much?" Monkey asked, still grinning. "Riker launched over Darlene and swung Roadie over his back before landing on him with a kidney punch. We didn't hear what he said, though."

"I want to know," someone said.

"Yeah. Roadie looks about ready to vomit or shit. What'd he say, Roadie?"

"Fuck off," Roadie snarled. He picked up his phone that must have fallen out and stormed from the room.

Riker tipped his head back, knowing I was already staring down at him.

"What'd you say?" I asked softly as the others, except Spade and Monkey, went back to partying.

He shrugged. "All I said was that I'd cut off his hands and shove them up his ass if he ever touched a woman like that again. And that I'd always be watching. Now I'm in your life, I've taken the women under my legs, and I'll protect them from bitches and manhandling. Especially if I see a woman wince like Darlene did."

"Don't you mean wings?" Spade asked.

Riker's brows dipped. "What?"

"Taken the women under your wings instead of legs."

"No. I have legs. I've never had wings and I won't."

His serious and confused face was adorable.

Riker glanced off toward the door where Roadie disappeared into. Obviously, his mind had drifted elsewhere when he asked, "I can't hurt him more, can I?"

"If he doesn't listen to your warning, you can."

He grinned. "I do get to keep an eye on him?"

"You do."

He went to his tiptoes, kissed my jaw, and skipped over to the women. "Come, come, my lovelies. You need to take my number in case any of you need my help." He paused and turned his head slowly to glare at Marker who was talking to Boff. They must have felt his stare because when they looked at him, they sneered.

Anger punched me in the gut.

"Mark, Boff," I called, and their gazes swung to me. I shook my head. Boff dropped his head and walked off while Marker tried to stare me down. Eventually, he clenched his jaw and headed over to the bar.

"I'll keep an ear out," Monkey said as he slapped me on the back and stalked off.

"I'm gonna go talk to Coms," Spade said. "I'm sure you wanna get outta here."

"Yep. Keep me updated. I'll come in when needed."

"You got it. Good to see you content, brother."

I tipped my chin up. "Thanks." After he walked off, I

waited, watching Riker and thinking that I had a good group of close brothers who I knew would be my ride or die and had already accepted Riker and me.

They knew I'd do anything for them. Like they would for me. That shit filled me with pride and gratitude. It wouldn't only be them either.

Once the rest had gotten used to seeing me with Riker and seeing what a good man he was, they wouldn't care it was a same-sex relationship. All right, there could be a handful who'd find it difficult to understand, which I'd eventually sort out, but for now, I just wanted to soak in the damn comfort of knowing I had good people in my life.

Just sucked I wouldn't be able to tell them anything of the new world I was now a part of, especially as I believed they'd support it. Well, after the shock of learning about everything.

Still, I wouldn't say anything unless I had permission. Riker's safety was too important.

Shaking the thoughts away, I called, "Riker."

He spun my way excitedly, then waved back to the women. "Got to go, ladies. See you next time." He raced back over to me and took my hand in both of his as I led us out of the compound. "You good if we drop into your place to grab some clothes for you?"

"I'm very good with that idea. And Rio will be cooking dinner about now so can we eat with them. That's if my brothers don't annoy you. They can be a bit much."

"As long as they don't hurt you, I'll have dinner with them."

"They've only ever shot me or stabbed me." A fire burned through my veins. I pulled him to a stop, and he hesitantly added, "Nothing too bad."

"Nothing too bad?"

"Yes?"

"Maybe they need to be shot and stabbed—*Oof.*" Riker's body hit me hard as he jumped at me. Thank fuck, I managed to wrap my arms around him before he fell. Though, he was clinging to me good and tight. "What are you doin'?"

"You make my dick so damn hard with all your talking and looks and how you watched me before you left for your meeting. My dick also loves how you commanded the room. How you didn't yell at me for teaching your brother a lesson. But most of all, my dick loves how you're not scared of my brothers who can do what they do and have the jobs that we do. It's all the freaking biggest turn on and my dick would very much appreciate that sucking sometime soon. That's why we won't stay long at my house."

Laughing, I pushed my face into the crook of his neck and kissed there. I pulled away to say, "We'll stay as long as you like. But your dick doesn't have to worry it'll get attention. It just may not be any good since it'll be my first head job for a guy."

"I have confidence in you," he told me seriously, then grinned. "Besides, I really don't mind being the one to lick you like a lollipop since I can come from that too."

"Jesus. Get in the car, sunshine. The sooner we get this done, the sooner we get back home."

"You got it." He tried to get down, but I squeezed his ass, which brought his gaze back up to me.

"First you gotta kiss me."

He smirked. "I do?"

I didn't answer. Instead, I leaned forward and took what I wanted. What I needed since it wasn't only his dick that'd been hard most of the time since being here.

He wasn't only going to suit me, but the club as well, because he already looked out for those who couldn't protect themselves. I loved my club. My brothers. But I also knew that some of them could get carried away. Could be a little rough and demanding.

Spade, Monkey, Coms, and I controlled what we saw or set to fixing what we heard. It'd still be good to have someone like Riker who the women had warmed to instantly. It looked like they already trusted him more than any of us, even when they knew they could come to me for anything.

CHAPTER EIGHT

RIKER

"**H**oney, I'm home," I yelled from the front door. I tugged Corbin in after me and down the hallway. I knew everyone would be in the kitchen area.

"No one's here," Nox called.

Laughing, I glanced back at my mate to see his scowl. My fox and I really loved how protective he got. My brothers were like that, but nothing like Corbin since he also wanted to save me from my annoying brothers.

I would have loved to have thrown them under the bus some more for shooting and stabbing me, but I really was at fault and had been looking for a fight at the time.

Hmm, maybe I should have told him that.

Stopping, I turned and pushed against his chest. "I should have maybe mentioned that it wasn't my brother's fault for stabbing and shooting me. I pushed them to react by talking about their fated."

He dipped down where his nose touched mine. "No fuckin' excuse, Riker."

"But I'm a shifter. We heal super speedy. I can show you. I'll go get one of my knives and—"

My hair was pulled back so fast, it stung.

My body melted and I grinned up at him.

"You ever think about stabbin' or shootin' yourself to prove somethin' to me, I'll be livid, sunshine. And when I'm filled with fury, it means we ain't fuckin' or suckin'. But also, no huggin', no touchin', no kissin'."

Pouting, I added in a glare since I was melty, wanted my way, but also annoyed he would keep those things from me. "Fine. I won't. Just don't be peeved at my brothers for something I led them into."

His jaw clenched.

"Please?" I tried.

He sighed. "I'll try not to be." He released his grip, and I hugged him close.

"Thank you." I took his hand again and we walked into the kitchen. Nox, Kieran, Deacon, and Rio were all there. "Hi, everyone. This is my fated, Corbin. But you have to call him Razor. Only *I* get to call him Corbin because it's something special. He's the one who kidnapped me to save me." I stepped to the side, holding his arm up so he was on display more. "Isn't he hot and awesome?"

Kieran cleared his throat and pushed his eyeglasses up. "I don't think we'll comment on his looks or awesomeness, Riker."

I hummed and nodded. "Probably best. Corbin won't like it if I get stabbed or shot again."

"Maybe it's also best if we don't keep bringing up the...." Rio made a gun with his hand and then stabbed himself with his invisible knife into his chest.

I looked back to Corbin to see he was having a stare down with my brothers. I nodded. "True, true." How did I defuse this situation? Did I really want to? Maybe it would be best if they just fought it out.

No. I didn't want my mate hurt.

I wasn't so worried about my brothers.

I mean, I was. I never wanted them dead. Never. We were a family.

Sighing, I moved into Corbin, and he wrapped an arm around my shoulders while I circled both of mine around his waist. I glowered at my brothers and mentally told them to quit looking at him with their coldness. If not, I'd let Corbin stab and shoot them.

"What's for dinner?" I asked.

Food was always good to lessen tension. It did for me anyway.

"I have something to say first," Corbin said. He glanced from Deacon, who sat at the table, to Nox, who stood behind Kieran where he sat at the counter. "Either of you injure Riker in any way, I don't give a fuck if you and your animals can rip me apart, I'll still be comin' for you and I'll have your blood."

When Deacon and Nox kept silent, I looked to Rio for help. He stared at us blankly before he went back to cutting some meat.

Great, he was too interested in getting dinner ready

than assisting in stopping a slaughter. I mean, usually I would like a bit of murdering before dinner, but not when it came with my mate.

Kieran clapped his hands. "Nox" was all he said.

Nox sighed. "Welcome to the fucking family. Threaten me again and I'll—Jesus."

Kieran elbowed him in the gut. "You were doing so well."

Deacon snorted as he picked up a dinner knife and touched the pointy end with his finger before he waved it around. "Welcome, *Razor*. It'll be good to get to know you."

"Yay, everyone is getting along extremely well. This is a splendid time. I think I'll grab my clothes and we'll go—"

"Sit down and eat with us."

Spinning, I launched myself at Mom. "Mom."

She cupped my cheeks and smiled down at me. "Hello, sweetheart. I'm so happy for you, and he is very handsome."

"How long were you listening, Ruth?" Nox asked.

Mom ignored him and turned to Corbin, holding out her hand. "It's a pleasure to meet you, Razor. I'm Ruth, the mother. Please ignore the other two idiots I raised and stay for dinner."

Corbin smirked. "Sure. I'd like that as long as Riker wants to."

Oh my God. He wanted to check with me. We were a partnering pair. An amazing fated mate bond. I couldn't wait for us to connect.

"I'd like to," I told him. He nodded.

"No knife throwing or shooting at dinner," Rio announced.

"After dinner?" Deacon asked with a grin.

"No. Besides, I doubt Riker will get as bored as usual. Which always led him to look for a fight to begin with."

Corbin turned back to me. "You stirred up trouble because you were bored?"

"Didn't I say that before? I'm pretty sure I mentioned something like that. And you were like, 'Oh, Riker, I don't mind as long as you keep staying as cute as you are.'"

Corbin scoffed. "Yeah, that sounds like me."

I nodded. "It really was."

"What else do you know, Razor?" Mom asked as we went to the table to sit down.

Corbin sat at the other end of the table with Mom and me on each side of him. "Only that Riker and his brothers are shifters. I'm Riker's fated mate like Rio is for Deacon, and Kieran for Nox."

"Sweetheart, do you mind if I tell Corbin a little more?" Mom asked.

"Go for it. He's accepted everything else really well. We haven't completed the bond yet, but I'm sure we will soon. He wants me for as long as we live."

"I can't say enough how happy I am for you." Mom smiled.

"Riker, why don't you go and pack some of your things," Deacon suggested. "Not everything. You'll want to come back here to live eventually."

"Of course...." I slouched. "Well, that's if it's okay with Corbin." I shifted my attention to him. "I know we haven't spoken about living arrangements, and I can understand why you wouldn't want to with Deacon and Nox here. But things will get better. I won't annoy them as much now that I have you." I frowned. "I could annoy you, though." I didn't like the thought of being annoying to the one person I'd love with my whole heart and soul.

"Riker, come here," Corbin ordered. As I got up, he scooted his chair back and pulled me onto his lap. I didn't straddle him or my dick would get ready for some action. Only now that I was thinking of action with my mate, my prick jerked under my jeans.

Corbin cupped the side of my neck. "We're a team, which means we're in this together, and the key is communication. I know there'll be times I annoy you. When I do, I want you to come to me to talk about it. Vice versa. Now, I ain't sayin' you will get on my nerves. But there'll be times when tension is high, and shit can happen. No matter what it is, we can work around anything that comes our way as long as we're honest. I never want you to change, though. Being you and stayin' you is important to me. If I do or say anything that hurts you in here"—he pressed a hand against my rapid heart—"tell me. Honesty, yeah?"

It made sense. I'd heard my brothers with their mates have heated conversations when they didn't agree on something. I'd just have to try my best not to take things to heart if we did get into an argument and he said something that upset me. I already knew he wouldn't mean it, and if something did happen, it'd be in the spur of the moment when things could get crazy.

I leaned my chest into his. "I promise to always be honest."

He smiled, running a hand through my hair. "Thank you, sunshine."

My body tingled at his petting, and I wanted to relax into him more, but I also had to talk about where home would be for us. I didn't mind if he wanted to stay at his house. I would miss my family like crazy, and sometimes it was easier to leave for work with them or on missions. But I didn't have to be here if my mate didn't want to be. "Um, what about the living arrangements?"

"I like where I am, but you work closely with your brothers, so I get why it's convenient. Plus, this place is big enough that I won't have to see them all the time. I'm happy with wherever you want to live."

"Really?"

He grunted with a nod. "Really."

So many emotions slammed into my chest, and I buried my face into Corbin's chest with a sniffle. I wouldn't cry. I didn't cry. The last time was after....

Yet my face felt wet.

Corbin's arms tightened around. His chin brushed over my hair. "What's this, sunshine?"

I shook my head.

I couldn't say it. I wouldn't.

But I had to.

He needed to hear it. He needed to understand that he meant so much to me.

"I never thought I could have something so precious, so special because of the things I've done, because my family never wanted me. They hated me. They showed me that hate through harsh words and punishments that messed with my mind. Torture that continued daily until

I was six. That's when I killed them all. And for ending their lives, I thought I wouldn't be lucky enough to have my very own fated mate. Someone who would be just for me. A person who would see me as me and accept everything I am now. When my brothers met their fated, I hoped and hoped and hoped. Then you walked into my life. I know we might fight. I know things won't be perfect, but to me, they already are because you're here."

I fisted my hands into his tee, under his vest, and pushed my face into his neck.

A trickle of fear raced through my veins at the thought of Corbin shoving me aside after learning I killed the family I'd been born to.

I wouldn't do it to the one I had now. I loved them. They loved me. But most of all, I loved my mate with my whole being.

His arms loosened from around me, his hands ran up my back, and he threaded some fingers through my hair.

With a tug, my head was away from his chest, and I blinked up at him.

"There's no one left to kill in your family?" he asked, low and harsh. The anger burning within him had my heart racing.

Mom sniffed off to the side.

Deacon grunted.

"No one," I told him.

His jaw ticked. "Know you can take care of yourself, sunshine, but know that from now on, I'll have your back. No one will get to you through me. You call me comin' into your life a gift and somethin' precious when it's the other way around. My life was dull compared to the night

I swept you outta that place, and you graced me with your color. I ain't givin' that up for anythin'." He tugged me closer, nose to nose. As I exhaled, he added, "Nothin' you've done in the past will change this for me. And we'll work on our future together to make sure we have as much time with each other as possible."

My stomach fluttered. "Corbin," I whispered, trying to control the burst of devotion inside me as I glided my palms up his chest.

His gaze flicked to my family while he said, "Thanks for the offer of dinner, but I'm changin' our minds, we'll do it another time." His attention went back to me. "Go pack, sunshine. I wanna get goin'."

Nox snorted, clearly reading what I already had with his luscious scent of arousal.

He didn't care my family was there witnessing this. He drew me in and kissed me. I opened up to him, needing his taste. His tongue slid, swiped, and tussled with mine.

A whimper escaped me, and someone cleared their throat.

Corbin pulled away and glared to the left for a moment before his attention was on me again.

He squeezed me to him, and ordered, "Pack your shit."

Grinning, I nodded. "You got it, Sir." I slipped off his lap and skipped out of the room quickly because I had a feeling our bond would be completed at his house.

Yay!

CHAPTER NINE

CORBIN

I'd watched Riker leave with a smile in place. I had to keep a lock on the fury pushing at me to hunt down the graves, to piss on them, of those who tormented him when he was a kid. Pride had settled under my ribs at knowing he killed them all, but I couldn't help the annoyance that there was no one left for me to take on.

Hell, I couldn't even be pissed at the brothers he now had since, under Ruth's watch, they'd accepted him, cared for him, and watched over him.

Although, the anger over them shooting and stabbing Riker easily surfaced. I hated the thought of anything harming him. Even if he could heal better than humans.

"If Riker slips up and says shit that annoys you or gets your animals pissed, you come to me to take care of it from now on," I said, dragging my gaze from the doorway Riker had gone through to Deacon and Nox. "I don't give a fuck if he can heal. No one hurts him. No one makes him bleed. You have an issue, talk to me, and I'll sort it."

All of them stared at me. The mates gaped, but the brothers' scowls were gone and instead, I wasn't positive, but they seemed to be considering me in a different light.

It was Ruth who shocked me. Hell, she even startled me when she threw herself at me and hugged.

I awkwardly patted her back when I heard her sniffle.

"Thank you. Thank you, thank you. Oh my God, thank you." She pulled back and cupped my cheeks. I watched as her tears welled and fell. "You really are the best person for our Riker."

I bristled at her calling Riker theirs.

He was mine.

I patted her arm, hoping she would release me. She didn't. Ruth sniffed again and said, "If you ever need anything, please don't hesitate to ask."

"Ruth, I don't think Corbin's exactly comfortable with you being in his face," Rio called.

She ignored him. "I always worried someone would take advantage of him. He's kind and trusting, even after everything that happened. But I know you'll be good for him, you—"

"Mom, please back off," Riker said tightly. His hard gaze was partially hidden by wet strands of his hair.

Ruth stepped away and clasped her hands in front of her, smiling softly at her son.

Riker's tension swept away on a snicker as he brushed

his hair back with a hand. "I guess I will get prickly when my mate is concerned because I was about ready to tear your eyes out, Mom." He skipped over to my side and dropped a bag to the floor. "Even when I love you, I was ready to throw hands for being in his personal space and touching him." Riker glanced to his brothers. "I get it now. Sorry for being a dick. Though, it was fun at the time." He laughed again.

Ruth hugged him before she went to sit down. "Sorry for getting too close to him, sweetheart. Are you sure you don't want to stay for dinner?"

"There'll be plenty of food," Rio said.

"And you might need the energy," Deacon teased as he tipped his chin up at me. I knew it was his peace offering. I supposed I couldn't be too stubborn since Riker didn't hate them. I hesitantly returned the gesture. Still, I'd keep an eye on both of them.

"But we understand if you have to go," Kieran put in, his cheeks turning pink.

Nox wrapped his arms around Kieran's shoulders and ducked to whisper something in his mate's ear that had Kieran's blush spreading.

Yeah, I didn't want to know or care what that was.

Standing, I curled Riker into my side and drew in his fresh, clean smell.

A pressure of urgency rose inside me to get Riker home. I needed to be inside him, have his teeth sink into me while I emptied my cum into him to complete this bond.

I didn't want to go another day without locking us together.

He had to know I wanted him, and I was in this for life.

It didn't matter we hardly knew each other. That shit would come. Fate picked us for each other. I knew I was meant to be with him to show him love and acceptance like no one else could, and he completed me in other ways.

Riker. Was. Mine.

And we had things to do. Mainly each other. So we wouldn't be staying.

Next time, I wanted to see Riker's room. I wanted to know where our space would be for when I moved in with him. But for now, I needed to get us out of there and home for privacy.

Leaning down, I picked up his bag and threw it over my shoulder. "Thanks for the offer, but we'll grab somethin' on the way back to my place."

"Bye, bye, everyone," Riker called brightly.

There were a chorus of "byes" as I managed to get him back outside, where night had fallen, and into the car without any delays.

When I was in the driver's seat, Riker faced me, grinning wild and widely. "What's the hurry, hunny-lumpkin?" He cackled when I screwed up my face at his choice of pet name.

My lips twitched as I started driving and tried to hold in a chuckle. "First off, it's a no to that name, sunshine. You can keep tryin' or I'm happy with sir."

He scrapped his top teeth over his plump bottom lip. I dragged my gaze back to the road.

"I like sir. I'd like to use it more when you're controlling me in bed. When you're choking me, fucking me, ruining my hole."

Jesus motherfucking Christ. A wave of arousal thickened my cock. I gripped the steering wheel, so I didn't pull over, park, and have him riding me then and there.

"Gonna fuck you when we get to the house, Riker," I stated roughly.

A noise, almost like a purr, rattled his chest as he rolled out a whispery, "Yes, please."

Another wave tingled along my spine and spread through my lower gut.

I pressed my foot on the accelerator. I hadn't been this fucking turned on where, even at my age, I worried I'd come in my pants.

But Christ, I had to touch him.

"Get your dick out for me. Wanna see if you're hard."

His noise amped up. He moved to lift his hips and force his jeans and underwear down to his thighs.

His erection sprang free and before he could touch it, I had my hand wrapped around him. He let out a shuddering breath around the noise still vibrating his chest and peered up at me through his lashes.

Goddamn, he was stunning.

As I ran my palm up and down his length, he gripped the sides of the seat, arching his back.

"Sir," he whispered, his tone full of desire. Legs spread, hips jutted up, he pressed his back into the seat and panted as I jacked him off.

My gut tightened in annoyance when I had to divert my attention from Riker to the road. Back and forth it went while all I wanted was to just stare at him. Watch how he lost himself to my touch, to the approaching orgasm.

He bit his bottom lip, and when I glanced back to him again, I noticed blood welling on it before it tipped over, running down his chin.

"Riker," I clipped.

His tongue swept out and swiped over his blood. His eyes closed and he moaned.

Fuck.

I pulled the car over, put it in Park, and undid my seat belt so I could use my other hand to drag his head my way to take his mouth in a metallic, heavy, and hard kiss.

He shuddered. I fingered and played with his balls, drawing them down from his body, noting he was close. Then I went back to jacking him.

My own cock throbbed for attention just before a hand ran up and down it over my jeans. I released his hair to lay my free hand over his.

I tore my mouth from him and nipped at his ear. "I ain't comin' in my jeans, sunshine."

He moaned and then offered, "I could lick you clean after."

Christ. That was tempting.

The thought had me jerking him faster. His eyes rolled, and he moaned again before muttering, "Corbin."

I nipped and suck at his earlobe. "Later, gonna have you full of my cum, sunshine. But right now, I want yours. I wanna see you messy, knowin' I caused it. Knowin' you loved my hand, my touch, my attention. Fuckin' come, boy, so I can get inside you faster."

His hand tightened over my junk, and he slammed his

eyes down to my hand working him over in time to see the first shot of his cum land on his tee. More erupted with his cry of pleasure. It dribbled down over my skin, his cock, his thighs.

When he tipped his head back with a dreamy smile, I kissed him lightly and licked over his lips.

"Don't make yourself bleed again, Riker. Unless I ask you to. Hear me?"

His cock twitched in my hand, trying to come to life again. "Yes, Sir," he breathed.

"Good." Releasing my hold on him, I grabbed some wipes out of the glove compartment, cleaned my hand, then ran some over Riker, getting most of his mess with a smug smile.

My cock throbbed once again. I really needed to lose my load, but I didn't want to until I was buried deep inside my sunshine.

The rest of the drive took too long. I was tight with tension and desire. I *needed* to get my hands on him. They twitched at the thought of marking his ass with a red haze from my palm.

How could I get it to work? How could I get Riker to misbehave?

When I got through the front door, I dumped his bag beside the couch, took off my cut and placed it carefully over the back.

Turning, I crossed my arms over my chest. "Run, little fox, because when I get you, I'll have you and I won't be gentle."

He made a small yip with an excited jig before he dashed off down the hall. I pulled my tee off on the slow walk to my bedroom. I undid my belt and slid it from my jeans, depositing it on the floor with a clank before I stored my wallet, keys, and gun in the drawer of the stand and locked it. I'd move my weapon to a better spot later, when I wasn't fighting with the burning hunger I had for Riker.

Slipping the key into my pocket, I walked down the hall as I undid the button and zipper of my jeans.

Inside my room, I removed my boots and socks as I eyed Riker sitting on the end of the bed, still clothed.

"Give me a safe word, Riker."

He squirmed and grinned. "Foxy."

"I want you to promise me to use it if you don't like somethin' I do or if you're in pain that's not pleasure."

"But I can take—"

"It ain't about what you can take. I don't want to cause *my mate* any pain that you don't like. Please, sunshine, for me. Be honest, even in the bedroom."

"I promise to tell you, my mate," he said softly.

I knew that when his gaze had flared over me calling him my mate for the first time that it meant something to him.

Good.

I'd wanted it to be special because I needed him to listen to me about this. I never wanted him in pain in any form. Not from me. Not from anyone. The thought of something happening to Riker had me swallowing fast as my gut churned.

"Get undressed, boy," I ordered to change the direction of my thoughts.

He cocked a brow and cheekily asked, "And what if I don't?"

Turned out, I didn't have to do anything for Riker to act up. My sweet sunshine wanted a punishment as much as I wanted to deliver one.

Smirking, I stalked toward him with a damn thrill in my lower gut at my eagerness to teach him a lesson.

CHAPTER TEN

CORBIN

I swept Riker up from the bed before I sat and threw him over my lap. Using one arm, I held his upper body down, then jerked his jeans low, which was easy since they were still undone. Once exposed, I ran my hand over his smooth ass cheeks that had a dusting of freckles.

"Is this what my boy wanted for talkin' back? For questionin' me?"

Riker nodded and panted. He rolled his hips forward, looking for friction on his hard dick that lay against my thigh.

Slap.

"Didn't say you could seek pleasure, boy."

He whimpered but turned to look up at me, biting his lip and grinning around it.

Slap.

The grin vanished when he moaned loudly and dug his fingers into my flesh at the back of my thigh he lay over.

I gently glided my palm over his red ass to ease the sting.

"More, Sir. Please."

"When I'm ready," I told him.

Slap.

Guess I was ready. I liked seeing my handprint on his ass. He whimpered some more. I brushed at the mark and then slid two fingers up and down his crack.

"*Please.* Please, Sir."

Slap.

He cried out. I eased the sting for a beat before I brought my hand up to spit on two fingers. I pulled his cheeks apart and ran the wet digits over his pink hole that tightened when I touched it.

I'd fucked women in the ass, so I knew what I had to do to prepare someone for it. But I never had the chance to play with a guy's hole where the prostate could deliver a more intense orgasm.

I wanted to see Riker come undone. Filled with so much pleasure he'd dream about it, so I'd be in his waking and sleeping hours.

Obsessed. The best word to describe what I felt for this boy panting on my lap.

I pulled his cheek aside to spit over his hole and pushed a finger inside his warm tunnel.

His groan was dirty and loud.

"More," he begged.

Adding another finger, I pressed, rubbed, and knew I located the right spot when his back arched and he moaned loudly. Hell, I felt his cock throb against my thigh.

However, the spit wasn't enough. I needed lube.

Removing my fingers, I grinned when Riker mewed in complaint. I tapped his ass and ordered, "Up. Get naked."

"No," he whined. "Put your fingers back—" His words cut off to a gurgle when I wrapped my hand around his throat and forced him up off me.

Standing, I tightened my grip, watching his face turn red. His lips parted, and his gaze darkened with that higher spark of arousal from being manhandled.

"Wanna fuck you with my cock, boy. You gonna do as I say to get my dick in your tight little hole?"

I let go when he leaned into me, running his hands up my chest. "Yes, Sir." He kissed above my nipple and moved away to tug his clothes off.

I went to the bedside table and got the lube out, putting it on the mattress.

When Riker stepped close, I picked him up and threw him on the bed. He bounced back with a laugh. Then scrambled to watch where I walked to the end of the frame.

"Spread 'em, sunshine. Show me where you want me. Show me where I know I'll only ever be from now on."

"Corbin," he whispered as he bent his knees and widened his legs for me. Feet planted on the mattress, hole on full display, it tightened from my stare. "It's yours."

"Only mine," I growled.

He whimpered and nodded.

Knees to the bed, I crawled up until I could breathe in his scent at his groin.

Fuck.

I was thirsty to try my first cock.

Kissing and nipping, I trailed my mouth up to suck him down my throat. He cried out my name, hands fisting my hair. Another thrill raced down my spine and pulled at my balls.

Since Riker's dick was a bit smaller and thinner than mine, I choked only a little when I forced him down the back of my throat and swallowed around him.

My dick leaked and soaked the bedding, knowing he loved my licking and sucking from the noises he made and how he moved. Arching, relaxing, squeezing me between his legs. Hands fisted and released.

"Sir, please, please, please."

I pulled off. "What do you need, sunshine?"

He grumbled when he saw my smirk, then answered, "You. In me. Filling me up and coming deep inside so I'll leak your cum for days."

"Fuckin' hell. I'd like that, seeing your ass wet from my cum still in you. I'd have to make sure I top you up all the damn time." I scooted up his body, biting and licking over his stomach, his nipples, chest, shoulders, and neck.

I rested back on my knees to stare down at his hole.

"Gotta stretch you more." I grabbed the lube, squirted some onto my fingers, and teased his opening before pushing in.

"No. I'm ready. I'm more than ready. My hole is aching for you."

"Know that, sunshine, from the way it's sucking my fingers in. Greedy little hole likes to be filled."

"Then fill me with your cock," he snarked. "Sir," he added when I cocked a brow. "*Please.*" He gripped the sheets while I fucked his hole with my fingers. I didn't want to give in just yet. I liked the feel of him. The squelching sound my fingers made with the lube.

My precum was near dripping from my cock, and I ached to be in his heat.

I pulled my fingers free to lube up.

"Yes, my mate." He sat up and ran his hands up and down my chest and stomach. He drove me wild for his touch, his taste. I pushed him back with a snarl, which had him cackling, but only for a moment. I threaded an arm under his ass and lifted, stuffing a pillow there. Leaning over him, with one palm to the bed, I took hold of the base of my dick and rubbed the tip to his hole. I spread around the lube and my precum.

He'd be soaked in my scent by the end of it, and hell, I wanted to pound my chest at the knowledge every shifter or other supernatural would know he was mine.

Pushing in, I watched the knob of my cock slip past the tight ring.

"Corbin," Riker complained, and I had no doubt it was because I was going slow.

"Like seeing your hole drink me down slowly, sunshine."

He let out a huff and glared up at me.

With a thrust, I buried my cock into his strangling heat with a groan.

"Yes!" Riker screamed, clawing at my arms and back,

knowing they'd scratch me up. I didn't care, though. I was busy trying not to lose my load within the first fucking second. Grinding my teeth together, I breathed through my nose.

Riker's ass clenched around me.

"Fuck," I clipped. Drawing back out, I thrust in again. He surrounded me like no other had. "Christ," I bit out.

"Hmm, fuck me hard, hunny-lumpkin."

"What did I say about names?" I demanded, lightly tapping his cheek before I gripped his throat. He hummed under his breath, arching his neck for me. Squeezing, I fucked in and out, faster and harder. My gut tingled from watching his lips part, eyes roll and close before they snapped open where I saw something else in there with him.

"*Mate*," he snarled, and suddenly, I was rolled to my back and Riker was bouncing hard on my dick.

"Like fuck," I growled.

Grabbing a fistful of his hair, I tugged, and he slowed.

Picking him up, I forced him to his stomach before I slipped my cock back into his ass and pounded into him.

He moaned as I wrecked his hole with hard slaps of my hips. He tugged my arm under his head. I kissed and licked over his shoulder and the back of his neck. His salty sweat tasted like a treat on my tongue. I wanted more and more.

"So good," he chanted.

I pulled back, gripping his hips to look down between us, to see my cock going in and out of his warmth. His walls snugged around me.

Christ, I was close.

"Corbin," he whined and then whimpered. "Coming."

When I bit down on his shoulder, he cried out, and then clamped his teeth into my forearm as I emptied inside him with a groan.

Something slithered into my chest, wound around my heart, and locked into place.

Riker. He was now a part of me, like I was him.

Mated. Connected. Bonded.

All of them.

Kissing and mouthing Riker's shoulder where I'd bitten him, I said, "I *feel* you."

When he turned his head, his eyes were teary, but I knew they were happy ones because he was beaming. "I feel *you*, my mate." He snickered. "In more places than one."

Grunting, I smiled. "Good."

I rolled off Riker to kneel beside him. Slipping a finger back inside, he shuddered.

"Soaked with me."

"Sir," he said on a moan.

Christ, I wanted to be back inside him. Feel his heat and tightness around me. Fuck my own cum and add some more.

But I needed to take care of Riker more, and I'd been hard on his ass. Removing my finger, I ignored his mew of complaint and got off the bed.

It was time to shower him, feed him, and, if he was good, maybe he could come again. But I'd have to change the sheets first since he'd already made a mess of them.

Grinning, I picked Riker up and threw him over my

shoulder. His cackle brought out my own carefree chuckle.

Hell, I couldn't even remember a time when I felt this content.

"RIKER, WATCH THE MOVIE," I said, kissing the top of his head.

He looked up and pouted. "Please?"

"Movie ain't done," I told him with a smirk.

We were sitting in the living room chilling after we'd showered, changed the covers to the bed, ordered and ate some pizza while we chatted about random shit.

Earlier, Riker had been rubbing himself up against me and running his hands over my chest, stomach, and boxers where my dick tented.

Which was why I made an excuse to use the bathroom and gone to the bedroom instead to get the lube. When I walked back out, I got Riker to sit on my lap. He'd started teasing my body with his soft touches again, and I'd slid my hand into his boxers to press my lubed fingers into his ass.

He'd sighed and relaxed for a while, just enjoying the feeling of a part of me filling him.

And fuck, I loved knowing that. It had me imagining stuffing him full of my fingers and cock all the time.

But now he'd touched my junk and had begged me to take him to bed to fuck.

"Corbin," he whined. "You washed your cum out of me. I need more." He grinned when my cock twitched. He quickly hid his smile by tucking his mouth down into his shoulder when I glared at him.

He dipped in to kiss my neck and picked up my arm to run his fingers over his bite mark, which he told me would scar. I'd wear it with pride. Already I wanted to show it off to anyone and everyone. Not many people would know what it meant, but we did, and that was all that mattered.

I pressed my fingers up, hitting the right spot and he quivered, squeezing his walls around my fingers.

"Gonna be obsessed with your ass as much as I am with you." I fucked my fingers in and out. He clutched at me, panting. "Listen to that wet hole. Jesus, sunshine, no matter the pounding earlier, you're still damn tight."

"Please," he whispered against my neck. "I'll be good."

"Don't need my boy good all the time. Like him wild. Like him dirty. Like you in a lotta ways, baby."

When my cell on the coffee table rang, I said, "Grab my phone, sunshine."

"Corbin," he whined, but he leaned forward, moaned when I pressed against his prostate, and shot back to lean his side into my chest. "Here," he snapped.

Taking the phone, I looked at the name. "Coms," I answered.

Riker gripped my arm when I resumed drilling his ass with my fingers, making sure I hit the spot that had him panting and nipping into my neck.

"Got some info on Writer. Only little shit at the moment but give me a couple'a days and I'll have more.

Then we'll make sure this fucker knows not to.... What the hell was that?"

It could have been Riker moaning into my neck.

"Nothin'. I'll—"

"Nothin'? Sounded like somethin', Prez. You got your guy ridin' your—"

Riker snatched the phone. "Hello, Coms. This is Corbin's guy. I wish I was riding something, but he's just teasing me. I can't stand it anymore. I need him inside me. I need—"

"Jesus. I suddenly want to wank," I heard as I took the phone back.

"You do it thinkin' of him, I'll fuckin' kill you." I hung up and threw the phone down while I withdrew my fingers, grabbed Riker, and threw him to his back on the couch. I had my dick out, his legs up on my shoulders, and I buried myself inside him. Both of us groaned, but it was Riker's smirk that had me whipping my hips back and forth harshly to punish his ass.

"You do not speak to a brother when your ass is full."

"Okay," he breathed. "Yes, harder, Sir. Oh, right there. You fuck me so good. *So* good." He cried out as he released all over his stomach and chest.

All it took for me to come with a groan through clenched teeth was the teasing lead up to my sunshine and watching Riker under me breathing heavily as he stared up at me in adoration.

Fuck, I loved this guy.

I didn't care if anyone thought I was crazy since we'd barely been together more than a day.

We were made for each other.

CHAPTER ELEVEN

CORBIN

I gulped my cold coffee and stared down at the table, cringing at the chatter around me. If I was with my brothers, I'd tell them to shut the fuck up. But I wasn't.

Instead of being in our cocoon of just us for a couple of days, our time was interrupted when Riker received a call about a job. Now I sat at the kitchen table in Riker's house with Kieran, his parents, and Ruth. Rio was in the kitchen again, half listening about wedding plans. They'd been at it a while, but before we got to this subject, they'd explained a few things about what it meant to be a fated mate when it came to the people surrounding me. My brothers. My club.

My body was still tense after discovering I'd age at a slower rate like Riker. That eventually we'd have to leave town and start somewhere else so people didn't question why we weren't aging. My gut had twisted over the thought of leaving the club and brothers.

Yet I would choose Riker over anything and anyone.

Knowing the club would be in good hands once Spade stepped into the president role helped ease the twisting to my gut over the news.

What also helped was knowing I'd be with Riker no matter where we went.

Maybe later, I'd consider more everything I'd learned, but it wasn't what was consuming my mind. It wasn't what had anxiety spiking.

Anger also pushed at me.

All of it was because I had to stay behind when Riker and his brothers got called out for work.

I swiped my hands down my thighs and gripped my knees, narrowing my gaze on the coffee mug that sat on the wooden table.

Lifting my head, I looked at Kieran who'd just pulled his hand away from patting my arm. "I'm worried too," he admitted.

"Same," Rio called.

Grinding my teeth together, I nodded.

"Sitting back and waiting never gets easy," Ruth said.

"That's what I don't get. Why the fuck do I have to sit back? I could help. I've done things like they do all the time when it comes to protecting people."

"I know you have, Razor. But you're not employed by our council. I'm not even sure Riker would want you in any danger—"

I thumped my fist on the table and leaned forward. "And you think I want him in danger?"

"Whoa, big biker guy," Kieran's father called as he stood with his hands up. "We're all a bit tense. You fated mates more so. But it's not worth taking it out on anyone."

Christ. He was right, and I already knew my actions were uncalled for toward Ruth. She'd be just as worried, being their mother.

But it seemed that the worry was getting to me that much more.

"Sorry," I muttered, jaw clenching.

Ruth smiled. "It's okay. I think—" Her phone rang, and she quickly snatched it up. "Hello?" She turned her back to us, but I saw the tension entering her. "Yes. ... Shit. ... I understand. ... No. I don't care what my fellow council members will say. We'll leave now, and everything will be fine. Keep an eye on the situation until we get there." She ended the call. "Razor, you're with me."

I stood, heart in my throat. "What is it?"

Kieran jumped up, too, and Rio moved around the counter.

Ruth raised her hands. "No one is hurt. There's a situation with the people the boys were sent after." She turned her full attention to me. "Riker is struggling because it involves children. This is something that we didn't expect. Deacon's worried Riker will lose it, and if that's the case, he needs his fated close."

I nodded. "Let's go."

She reached out to Kieran and Rio, taking their hands. "They'll need you when we get home."

Rio curled an arm around Kieran's waist and nodded.

"Of course," Kieran replied, tears welling, but I saw him steel himself as he drew in a breath.

When Ruth rushed from the room, I was right behind her.

Ruth slid into the driver's seat, which meant I had to take the passenger. "Tell me about the job."

"It was supposed to be a quick, easy in and out at a warehouse downtown. We had people watching one of the gangs in town. They'd made too much of a disturbance for us to leave them be. We weren't sure if it would come to ending lives tonight, but it sounds worse than we thought."

"What were these members doing that got the council on their radar?"

"They're small fries in trading with drugs and weapons. Nothing like the cartel or other clubs. But they caught our council's attention by robbing a few shifters' places. We thought they were targeting the shifters for a reason. Now, we doubt it, but we've still kept an eye out because their trade has been picking up lately. It's time to put a stop to their business dealings. They've also done some car lifting and burglaries. I don't understand why they would have children in there."

"What did Deacon say?"

"The children look malnourished and abused. How far the abuse has gone, we don't know yet."

Fuck.

"Do we go in when we get there? What's gonna happen?"

"We'll sneak in and see if we're needed and proceed

from there. You're armed. I know because I can scent it. Use it if you have to. If we get separated, protect your life at all costs."

Riker's would come first. Still, I tipped my chin up, not wanting to argue. "How'd Deacon call in the first place?"

"It wasn't Deacon on the phone. He relayed his message to Dash, who was keeping watch, and then asked him to call me. Dash is an elf we trust. He can speak telepathically."

An elf? Riker had mentioned other species, but I hadn't taken it in.

"With pointy ears and all?"

Ruth snorted. "Yes."

Fucking hell. An elf.

My world had just become a whole lot bigger.

Grunting, I rubbed my palms up and down my thighs. None of that eye-opening bullshit mattered right now. My only focus was making sure Riker came out of this situation okay. I was all too aware this could screw with him. I'd help in any way I could. Deacon and Nox had their fated mates to calm them later. I was it for Riker, and hell, I was glad we'd met so I could be there for him now.

Ruth pulled over and we climbed out. She pressed a finger to her lips, and once I nodded, we moved off toward a large brick warehouse.

Lights shone from within. Voices filtered out of the structure. We crept around the side to the long, thin walkway, which had a field to the left of it.

Why were there no guards outside?

Unless the gang found Riker and his brothers and

they were all inside. But wouldn't they keep someone on watch still?

A figure stepped out of some shrubbery. I had my gun out and pointed in seconds.

Ruth placed her hand over it as voices rose from inside the building.

I jolted when a voice slammed into my mind. *Ruth has asked me to connect you into our conversation.*

What had Ruth called him? *Dash?*

The elf nodded. *Yes, I'm Dashiell. A friend to your mate.*

Lowering my gun, I opened my mouth to reply until Ruth shook her head and tapped at her temple.

How do I even talk?

The corner of Dash's lips tipped up. *As you are now.*

Right.

Tell us both, Dash, Ruth sent through.

I didn't dare think of anything in case he could pick up on it.

I'm the outside assistance for the brothers. I've removed the foe surrounding the building. Deacon says Riker is close to losing himself because the men inside hold at least twenty young ones who they were going to sell.

My upper lip rose, gut knotting. *Fucking hell.*

Dash nodded, and I caught a glimpse of his pointed ears when his long black hair moved in the breeze.

You need to get in there, he continued. *Calm your mate before he slaughters everyone in front of those poor young ones. Get the children out, and then let the shifters have their fun. I'll stay out here for the little ones and make sure no more trouble comes.*

Thank you, Dash. Ruth patted his arm and turned to me. She pointed to a window and moved off. I nodded my thanks to the elf and followed quickly.

At the window, we stood on either side of it. Ruth took a quick look around before she jimmied the lock with a pocketknife she'd pulled from her pocket. Pausing, she frowned, and put the blade away. She pushed the window open with a shake of her head.

It hadn't even been locked. These idiots' mistakes were to our advantage.

I needed to get in there. I had to be near Riker.

Ruth slipped into the room first. She made it look easy, but she was smaller than me.

With a grunt, I lifted myself into an office. The room had drywall that went up from floor to waist height. The rest was made of glass. More offices lay to the left and right, and across from all rooms was a long hallway. Light from small glass panels at the top of the hallway lit the way. On the other side of the hallway wall was the room where the voices came from.

We sneaked out of the room, and I screwed up my nose from the mold smell permeating the air. The offices appeared unused and more like a storage area. Papers, bookshelves, and desks filled the rooms, but all held a thick layer of dust.

At the door leading out, Ruth pressed close and listened for a few moments before she opened it just a crack.

Voices grew louder.

"Like we've said a million times, leave without the children and you'll escape unharmed," Deacon called.

"That's not happening, motherfucker."

A child whimpered.

"Don't hurt her. Don't hurt her. Don't hurt her," Riker chanted.

Shit.

"Shut him the fuck up," roared an unfamiliar voice.

"You just need to leave, and no one dies." That didn't come from one of the brothers.

There was a snort, and then it was Nox saying, "Do you need us to use ASL to sign the same fucking words to you? We're not leaving without the kids."

Another whimper before the growling started.

"Riker. Still."

I pressed a hand to Ruth's back while she peered through the doorway. After a nod, she slipped through and I followed. Boxes were stacked across from the door we'd just come from, creating the perfect barrier that left us undetected. Free to go left or right, I studied both. Either could lead us into the open area of the warehouse.

We needed to split up.

Tapping Ruth's shoulder, I pointed to the left and waved her off to the right. Ruth shook her head and glared. I waved my gun around to remind her I would be safe from a bunch of fucking gang members.

Her lips thinned, and then she finally nodded.

She saw my smile, rolled her eyes, and walked off.

I stayed low so no one spotted me over the boxes and moved along behind them. The brothers and gang kept firing back words at each other, but I pushed it all aside to concentrate on my surroundings. I didn't want any surprises coming my way. I couldn't fuck this up. Riker's own sanity was at risk. If Riker decided to attack and kill in front of those kids, traumatizing them, that'd mess Riker up more than anything.

With the brothers distracting the gang, possibly make the idiots think they had the upper hand, it left me to sneak around easily.

At the end of the corridor stood a guy who looked like he could use a good meal and a shower. Low hanging jeans were loose on his hips, his chest bare. Scabs marred his back and arms. *Junkie.* He tapped his left hand on his thigh while he pointed a gun toward Nox, Deacon, and Riker, moving it over the three of them.

The brothers stood together on the far side where Ruth would be. I'd picked the area where the gang loitered. Also, on my side and close to the man in front of me, were the kids huddled together on the ground. Three other gang members surrounded them.

The rest of the gang stood around the man who was the clear leader. The asshole held a crying little girl in front of him.

How the hell was I going to get the kids out without the gang just shooting me?

Fuck.

Reaching out, I hooked an arm around the junkie's throat and pressed my gun to his temple.

He gripped my arm with his free hand before he choked and scratched at my arm. He wasn't fighting too hard, though, and at least the voices of the others still arguing blocked the struggle.

When I tightened my arm, cutting off his air supply more, he finally stilled.

"Lay your gun on the fuckin' floor quietly." I forced his stunned body to bend, and he slowly placed his gun to the concrete floor. I dragged him behind the boxes. He started to kick back and slap at me but lost consciousness in moments. I laid his body to the floor.

Straightening, I rolled my shoulders before I stepped back around the boxes. I noticed none of the gang members had even looked this way. They didn't realize they'd lost a member. But Nox and Deacon did. Hell, they likely heard me. Their glance was quick, though, not wanting to draw more attention my way.

I didn't think Riker had even registered.

Christ. They really were this stupid. Unless they were too doped up on their own product, remaining oblivious to someone approaching them from behind. Then again, they probably thought they still had men outside.

Didn't matter what it was.

I had to get this shit done.

"Just fucking leave" was screamed from their leader.

This was spiraling fast, the leader losing all control and composure.

As I strolled out further with my gun at my side, none of the gang that stood with the kids, looked my way. Everyone's attention was trained on the brothers.

A definite advantage for me.

Deacon noticed me and flinched with surprise. Maybe they hadn't recognized my voice and thought other help had shown. Nox was next, his brows rising. Riker, in human form, was too busy crouching and crawling in front of his brothers while watching the leader like he was prey.

I shouldered my way into the group around the leader and just before I reached him, others finally noticed.

Noise rose.

Voices yelled.

Someone tried to grab for me, and I dodged them.

Slipping behind the leader, I pressed my gun to his spine while wrapping my arm around his neck. I twisted us to face his members. Unfortunately, his grip on the girl didn't loosen.

Raising my gun, I tapped it against the leader's temple. "Tell them to back the fuck off and let go of the girl."

Cackling started. *Riker.* I flicked a glance to him. He now stood and grinned. When I moved my attention back to the gang, I heard clapping.

"Oh, hey, and yay, that's my man. He's *my* man. Come to save the day. It reminds me of when he kidnapped me. Shoot him, lover boy."

Relief flooded my body now that Riker's demeanor had changed. I could even see some tension drain from Deacon and Nox as their shoulders rounded.

My lips twitched. "Riker, what the hell did I say about pet names?"

Riker laughed wildly and clapped again.

"Drop the fuckin weapon, asshole," I ordered roughly when I felt him shift slightly. He didn't listen. He wouldn't listen. Did he think he still had the upper hand because of the kids around?

Fuck, he probably did.

Lowering the gun, I pushed it into the back of his upper arm covered by a dirty tee and fired.

Kids screamed.

He bellowed as he dropped the gun and let go of the girl to grab his arm.

"What the fuck? What the fuck? What the fuck?" he chanted, voice tight with pain.

"Go, girl," I barked, and she ran right toward Deacon, who scooped her up and placed her in Ruth's waiting arms.

The kids settled when they saw their friend out of harm's way.

I shook the leader in my hold. He moaned.

"Get your men to move away from the other kids," I demanded.

"Move," he whimpered.

As I backed us up, so no one was behind us or close to our sides, I hit the butt of the gun to the top of his head. "Louder."

"Fuck! Move. Get away from them."

"But—"

"Move," he bellowed when I tapped the gun to his temple again.

Slowly, they edged toward the area where I'd downed their other guy.

"Go to the men," I told the kids.

"Come on, children," Ruth called.

"Where's our guys outside?" someone asked.

"Shit, this isn't fucking good." The voice sounded panicked.

"We've got to get out of here," another all but cried.

"No one moves," I snapped.

The children stopped.

Sighing, I tipped my chin toward the brothers. "Except you lot. Go on now. Hurry," I told them.

They cried and sobbed as they raced toward help. We all watched in silence when Ruth led them behind the boxes. She'd get them safely to Dash.

When the last kid disappeared around the corner, I called, "Sunshine."

"Yes, Daddy Sir?"

Daddy sir? Hell, I didn't mind that at all.

"You after some blood?"

His laugh was lower than normal and cruel. "Oh, yes."

I released my hold and shoved the leader hard. He stumbled forward and fell to the ground. I dropped low as some fired their guns my way.

There was a snarl, rip, and suddenly Riker, in his fox form, was on the leader, tearing into his skin like it was paper. He bit, scratched, and tore.

I rolled and shot a member as he came at me. Nox took down the next few with his guns.

A roar sent shivers down my spine, and I glanced over to see Deacon as his huge bear chased after the ones running. His huge paws slapped loudly on the concrete.

Since I was somewhat safe as the carnage happened around me, I rested on my side with my head in my hand and watched the brothers work.

Riker was a magnificent sight to behold.

His fox had finished killing their leader and bolted for another. He ran up the guy's back and latched onto his neck. I went to get up when I saw the guy punching at my fox, but Riker released him and snapped at his hand, his shoulder, his jaw. The guy dropped to his knees and the fox slipped around to the front of the guy, ripping out a piece of his throat.

Maybe, just maybe, I wouldn't be as jittery as I was when Riker left for a job.

Seeing how they performed in a risky situation was better than hearing about it.

Though, I'd still offer up some help since they'd witnessed how I worked.

CHAPTER TWELVE

RIKER

"*I* know I keep saying it, but I really, *really* mean it. You were the sexist man I'd ever seen walking into that group like you owned the place," I told my wonderful, amazing mate once again as we drove back to his place after leaving Deacon, Nox, and Mom to deal with the rest. I already knew our job was done, but the council would get their detectives to investigate the gang more and find out who was behind their order to sell the poor little children.

I didn't want to think about them now, though. I'd just get mad, and there was no one left to kill.

Instead, I picked up my mate's hand, which was already in mine, and rubbed it against my cheek. We'd washed up at the warehouse before we'd headed outside. Even Corbin had a different tee on when I joined him. I hadn't wanted to scare the kiddies any more than they already were. If I walked out with blood and guts all over me, I would have. Luckily, Nox had stored a bag of our clothes outside when we'd first arrived.

I kissed and licked at Corbin's fingers. He was the bestest thing I could have seen in that moment in the warehouse when my hunger and need to hunt, hurt, and kill was at the snapping point.

Until I saw him.

Until he strolled on out like God's gift, and boy, was he a gift, and he handled that situation like a hero in a movie.

The kiddies were safe. They would be reunited with families because my mate had made it so.

"Glad you thought so, sunshine."

"I know my brothers were worried about me," I said, and added softly, honestly, "I was too. I thought I was going to lose it in front of them." I brightened at my next words. "But then I saw you and those darker feelings washed away. You brought me back." I kissed his knuckles and clutched his arm to my chest.

My fox chittered and purred inside me.

We were very grateful our mate was here.

"We need to fuck," I told him, and he chuckled. "I want to show you how happy it made me you were there."

Desire filled his eyes as he peered over at me with an electrifying heat. "It's good that we're heading to the compound, then."

"Why there?" I asked. People would want his attention, and he'd get distracted from me. I didn't want that. I needed him to fill me and fuck me hard.

Own me.

Control me.

Mark me.

"It's closer than my place, Riker. Seeing you fight and protect got me hard, sunshine. Wanna be inside you as much as you want me to be."

Slowly, I slid his hand down to cup my erection. "Can I call you 'daddy sir' again?"

"Anything you want, pretty boy."

My stomach rolled in the best way with tingles and sprinkles.

"Are we there yet?"

His laughter filled the car. I'd been surprised when Deacon gave Corbin permission to drive his toy. Although, my brother was happily surprised over my amazing mate.

"Soon," he said, squeezing my cock, making me pant out a breath.

"We could just pull over and you can fuck me."

"Your brother will kill me if we get jizz in his car."

"Outside?" I suggested. I wasn't picky where we were.

He squeezed again. "It's just up the road. How about you tell me what happened in there before Ruth and I arrived?"

"Boo, that's boring." I sighed. "But fine." I pulled his hand away from my prick so I wouldn't get distracted and played with his fingers while I told him, "We scouted the area for a while first. Called in Dash. Helped him get rid of the dickheads outside before we moved in. We thought we were dealing with a gang for other issues, but they'd stepped up their game and were looking at wanting to...."

My upper lip rose, and a growl rolled out. "Did you see their bruises?"

"The kids'? Yeah."

"They were hungry and thirsty as well. We could see it, hear it. They'd suffered all because those men wanted to sell them to who knows who."

"They're safe now," he reminded me, calming me by sweeping his hand out of both of mine to clamp it to the back of my neck. "Your council will find out who they were going to sell them to, and they'll send you and your brothers out to deal with them. No one who's willin' to buy a kid is good news."

"They're not."

"We'll find them. I know it."

I turned toward him. "You said *we.* Does that mean you want to assist us on jobs?"

He cocked a brow. "Would you want me to?"

"*Yes. Yes. Yes,*" I said, bouncing with each word. "I know you can take care of yourself. Plus, my brothers and I wouldn't take you on jobs where there'll be a lot of straight-up killing because you could get shot. We get shot all the time. We just heal quicker than humans. But if situations like before happen, I want you with me. I want you with me all the time, but just not on those deadly ones when we're all slaughter, kill, stab, bite right away."

He grinned. "Got you, sunshine, and that sounds good to me. I'd be happy to come help on jobs like that one. Before, when you were getting dressed, Ruth said she'd check with the council, but I think they'll let me."

I clapped as excitement bubbled in my stomach. "That would be amazing." Until a thought popped into my mind and my shoulders drooped. "But what about your club? Your brothers? Your businesses?"

He tapped my chin until I raised my head, and he placed his hand on my thigh. I wrapped both of mine around his again. "Don't stress, yeah? We'll figure it all out since it seems we have a long time together." He grinned.

"Ruth told you all about that?"

"Yeah, sunshine. I couldn't be happier to know I got more days to spend with you." He winked. "I know I'll have to leave the club and my brothers, but that ain't any time soon. I wanna enjoy what we have in our lives now and worry about that shit later. Though, I don't think leavin' will be too much of a worry. Got no blood family of my own to hold me here. They're all dead. Besides, I'll have you and my new family. A new club of our own. Besides, I know Spade will take care of the brotherhood like I do."

"Is it too soon to say I love you? Because I do. I love you. You've accepted me, my ways, my fox, my family, and gone with everything that's happened like the best person in my world. I-I never felt so much happiness in my chest" —I tapped there—"before, and I know you'll keep filling me with more. I'm sorry if it's too soon to say 'I love you' and it scares you off, but you're kinda stuck with me anyway now, with the biting and claiming and all, which means that if I did scare you and you run, I'll come after you. I'll find you. And I'll make sure to tie you to a bed to remind you that we can be perfect together."

My breaths panted out of me through my nose since I was biting down on my bottom lip in worry while thinking I'd said too much.

Corbin went back to killing the steering wheel with both hands. His jaw clenched. He also breathed hard through his nose.

I couldn't scent anything bad coming from him, so I wasn't sure what was going on in his mind, and our bond only connected our emotions *slightly*. I was sure he wasn't upset. But the doubt still wormed its way in.

Did I ask him to say something?

No, I shouldn't. I had to wait for him. At least I thought that was the case. I guessed when in doubt, it was good to stay quiet. Though, it was sooo hard—like my dick—to keep my mouth shut. I had to bite on my lips to keep myself from yelling at him to say something.

My belly knotted when the silence went on and on and on.

I pressed my hands to my stomach and waited, staring down at my bouncing knee.

The car suddenly stopped. Corbin turned it off, pushed his seat back before he reached over to me and undid my seat belt.

"What—" I let out a laugh when he pulled me onto his lap. My knees dug into the hard parts of his seat, but I didn't care.

Corbin cupped my cheeks and looked at me with intense eyes, which had me squirming on his lap.

"It ain't too soon, sunshine, because I'm right there with you in feeling this. Never loved anyone the way that I love you, Riker Blackwood. I'm glad to be stuck with you until the day I die, and I know I'll die happy because I've had you in my life. Fuck anyone who questions us, our love. No one else matters but you and me, baby. Love you."

He pulled me in and slammed his lips to mine. I scrambled to grip him, to hold him and return the hot, heavy, and hard kiss.

A kiss that felt like we wanted to devour each other. Like we couldn't get enough. Like we wanted to be buried inside each other.

The sting to my hair had me breaking the kiss to moan. Corbin tugged my head back roughly and kissed my neck, my shoulder. He bit there, and I rocked over his hardness. My own cock ached for release.

I needed him inside me first. I wanted to come while he stuffed me full.

A knock sounded on the window. I growled, and Corbin barked, "Fuck off."

He licked and sucked on my earlobe. I shivered.

Someone chuckled outside the car.

Corbin cursed under his breath and pulled away.

"No," I whined. "Can I kill them?"

Corbin grinned. "Not yet."

"Not at all," Spade said as he opened the door. "Hey, you've got someone watchin' from across the road. How about you pull the car in behind the fence?"

I glanced around and snickered when I realized we hadn't even made it inside the compound parking area. Corbin had stopped us just in front of the gates since he obviously couldn't wait to get his hands on me to let me know he loved me.

My belly whooshed.

I hugged him to me before I got out of the car.

"Hey," Corbin complained and tried to snatch me up, but I was quick. "What the fuck, Riker?"

"I'm going to see who was watching us without our permission."

"Does that mean you'd give permission to watch you two? Because fuck, I kinda want to watch from what I've seen and heard already," Spade confessed.

I grinned, liking the idea of showing Corbin off so Spade could see our love and how much my mate let loose in bed. Corbin snorted and shoved Spade out of the way when he climbed out of the car. "Not happenin', brother."

"That is a pity," someone called from the other side of the road.

I peered over and waved while bouncing up and down. "Soren. Hey. Hi." I skipped over the road.

"Soren?" I heard Corbin mutter as he and Spade followed.

When I stopped in front of Soren, I smiled and I hugged him tightly, which he returned before he pushed me back to cup my cheeks.

"Sweetheart, it's so good to see how happy you are," he whispered before the others arrived. "Dash told me more about your mate coming to help you. He's mighty, honey. I just wanted to check on you myself after the situation, but I can see you're in good hands."

"I am. He's the best there ever was. But thank you for checking on me." Just as I went to glance to see where Corbin was, a grip tugged on the back of my tee, and I was pulled away from Soren.

The scent of jealousy touched my nose.

"This is Soren who *loves* you?" Corbin demanded, curling an arm across my chest to bring my back into his front.

I nodded, my smile growing. "That's him." I liked knowing Corbin got jealous, but I didn't want any blood shed between my friend and my mate. "But he's only ever loved me like a brother."

"A little adorable brother who gets into trouble all the time," Soren teased.

"Yet you still love me."

His eyes softened. "That I do."

"Yeah, all right." Corbin held out his hand. "Name's Razor. Thanks for keepin' an eye out for Riker, but I've got it from here."

Soren smirked and winked. "I'm sure you do." He placed both hands around Corbin's as they shook.

I stared at their hands as Soren's flirty words ran through my mind over and over.

My upper lip rose. "Soren," I snarled.

Soren dropped his hands. "Forgive me, sweetheart. Your... fella is a sight to see. I'm jealous. I'd like one of my own."

A throat cleared.

Soren and I glanced at Spade as Corbin dipped down to kiss my neck, making me all melty.

My friend took a long look at Spade, running his eyes up and down him slowly. "Well, hello. We haven't been introduced."

Spade snorted. His hand came out. "Spade."

Soren shook it. "Spade. I like it. My name is Soren." When he pulled his hand away, Spade had a card within his. "My contact details are on there. Come by for a drink one night. If you're game." He winked and turned to me. "I must go, my sweets. I'm sure I'll see you both around." He bopped me on the noise. "It's a true treasure to see you glowing." He walked off to a car that started before he got in, and as soon as he was, it drove off.

Corbin suddenly snorted. I glanced up to see him looking at his friend.

Spade stared down at the card with bunched brows.

"You confused, brother?" Corbin asked.

Spade lifted his head. "That was him hittin' on me, right?"

Laughing, I nodded. "Yes, but he's leaving it up to you if you want to fuck him or not."

"Hell." He pocketed the card. "Ain't ever thought about being with a guy before, but that Soren was damn hot."

I nodded. "He gets men and women falling all over him all the time."

Corbin suddenly picked me up and threw me over his shoulder. "You better not be one of them, sunshine. You're all mine." He slapped my ass.

"Oooh, Daddy Sir, do that again when we're naked."

He turned and I heard the keys jingle. "Spade, drive the car in."

Spade chuckled. "You got it, Prez. Enjoy yourselves."

Grinning from over Corbin's shoulder, I waved to Spade as my belly fluttered and cock thickened.

We were definitely about to enjoy ourselves.

CHAPTER THIRTEEN

RIKER

"Hey, Prez—"

"Later," Corbin called to someone as we walked down the hall. The guy laughed. I lifted my head to see, but I didn't recognize whoever it was. I waved anyway, and he tipped his chin up.

"Razor." It was a woman's voice that time. "Don't worry, I can see you're busy."

Corbin grunted as we passed one of my new besties Lynnette.

"Hey, Lynnette. We'll be busy for the rest of the night."

She snickered. "I'll let everyone know not to disturb you."

"Thanks. I really don't want to hurt anyone if they do."

She saluted me just before we turned another corner. Corbin's big feet ate up the flooring with each pounding step. He opened a door at the end of this hall and stepped in, slamming it shut after us.

When he planted me on my feet, he gripped my hair and tugged my head back to take my mouth.

I moaned into the kiss, opening up to his tongue, and grabbing ahold of his tee. Until I pushed him away in the next moment to pull mine up and off me.

"Naked. Please, Daddy Sir."

"Boy, *you* get naked fast and grab the lube outta the top drawer over there."

Nodding, I removed my shoes and pants, and rushed over to the drawer, quickly taking in the room. It was like some of the hotel rooms I'd seen on TV. A bed, maybe queen, a desk, a set of tall drawers, and two bedside tables. There was another door beside the bed where the bathroom was. I could see the tiles through the crack.

The design of the room fled my mind when I grabbed the lube and turned to see Corbin standing in only jeans with his belt wrapped around his hand.

"Bend over the bed, boy."

A thrill raced up my spine, and I nearly tripped when I moved to get to the end of the bed. I grumbled under my breath but stopped when I pressed my hands to the mattress, glancing over my shoulder.

My daddy sir snapped his belt out as he watched my ass and then slid the length of the leather through his other hand in a leisurely stroke.

"Gonna mark you up, sunshine."

Pleasure weakened my knees. I locked them in place as I begged, "*Please.*"

Had to have them. His marks. Wanted to parade them around for everyone to see before they faded and he could give me some more.

They were just mine. He'd never mark anyone like he would me.

He knew I could take it. He liked that I wanted it. I could see the desire, the crave for it.

Whack

Arching, I dug my claws into the bed and moaned from the stinging pleasure sweeping through my body.

His hand ran over my cheeks, numbing them in a warm stroke.

Whack.

His palm glided over my sensitive skin again.

Whimpering, I panted out, "More, harder, Daddy."

Whack.

"Fuck." I drew out through a moan.

That one hurt, but my cock, leaking and aching, was on board. I wanted to jerk off, to come, but I didn't. I needed this to last longer.

My perfect, precious mate had to be inside me, filling me before I came.

"You're such a beautiful, special boy. My sunshine. Just mine." He kissed my shoulder, my back. My ass.

"Daddy," I breathed.

Two fingers ran up and down my crack.

I whimpered.

"Nox—"

I turned and snarled, flashing my upper teeth. "Why are you talking about my brother?"

Whack.

"Still," he ordered.

My mind cleared as pleasure soaked in again.

"As I was gonna say. Nox has tats, so I presume all shifters can get them."

I nodded and bit my bottom lip as he toyed with my rim.

"Want my name on you, boy."

A new thrill raced through my lower belly and balls.

I needed that.

I wanted that.

"Yes. Fae magic can make it stick. Dash will do it. Where, Daddy Sir? Where do you want your name?"

Fingers ghosted over my skin, shoulder to shoulder on my back. "Here. And one on your chest."

Both sides. So, no matter how he fucked me, he had a chance of seeing his claim.

My balls tightened, and I nodded. "I want. I *so* want."

I'd organize it as soon as possible.

Corbin leaned into me and sucked at my shoulder and my neck, drawing my blood forward. Heating me even more.

"Gonna get your name too. My sunshine. My Riker. My fox. Name across my heart. Fox image and the name sunshine on my neck."

My pulse quickened at the image of it.

"I want it. *Need* it. You already have my claim on your arm, but no one knows the reasons behind the bite. No one knows we own each other. People will see my name on your neck. They'll see the warning. They'll know that if they touch you, I'll kill them. I'll slaughter them to a point where no one will know what they looked like before."

His slick finger pushed inside me. I arched and moaned.

"Exactly," he whispered into my ear as he finger-fucked my hole. He bit my earlobe and sucked before he added, "And if they didn't see your mark, your name, and they messed with me, I'll stand back to watch you work them over. Then after you've dealt with them, we'll fuck with their blood coating our skin."

A growl fled from my mouth when my cock throbbed as a heady wave of desire licked at my skin. I blinked through a haze and pushed back on his fingers.

I wanted more.

I had to have him inside me.

Tightening my walls around his fingers, I met his stare and pleaded, "Daddy. In me, please."

Just "Daddy" or "Daddy Sir," I didn't care. I loved using both, knowing Corbin enjoyed hearing it from the wild flash in his gaze.

"Christ, you're stunning when you beg for my cock. Like a little starved slut for his daddy."

Nodding, I mewed and hummed and whimpered when he brushed his fingers over my magic button inside.

I panted like the best porn star, dazed with desire, hungry for his cock.

"If you want to play with my hole longer, let me suck you, Daddy. Please. Need more than your fingers in me."

He reached under me and fisted my aching cock. I

slammed my eyes closed and grunted. If he jerked me off, I'd come. I didn't want that yet.

Thankfully, he only held it as he fucked my ass harder and faster with his fingers.

"Daddy, close," I whined.

I lost his hands altogether and he stepped back.

"Hold that position, boy," he ordered as he stood at the side of the bed and undid his jeans. He kicked off his boots, removed his socks, and pushed the rest of his clothes off.

"Look at you staring at me like a hungry little cockslut."

Nodding, I licked my lips. Eyes trained on his hand as he palmed his erection.

"Daddy," I snapped low, another growl rattling out. My fox danced around inside me. He liked our mate's teasing, but I was frustratingly twisted up inside with so much arousal that I nearly vibrated from it.

I even considered humping the mattress when all Corbin did was smirk at me while he slowly jerked off.

Inch by inch, I moved my hips down, aiming for the edge of the bed to get some friction over my leaking and throbbing dick.

"Riker," he warned.

"Please, Daddy Sir. My hole needs to be fucked so bad. I have to have your cum filling me."

"Christ." He moved to the end of the bed where my ass was very much waiting and willing.

Yippee skippy.

I quickly hid my satisfied smile behind my shoulder.

Smack.

I jolted forward and cried out from his palm connecting with my ass before he rubbed out the sweet sting.

"Don't think you're gettin' your way with all the beggin', boy."

"I'm not?" I asked when I felt the tip of his cock press against my hole.

"It's only because I was sufferin' not being inside your heat. Need your greedy little hole stranglin' my cock."

Nodding, I spread my legs and dropped my upper body to the bed. "Stuff me full, Daddy Sir."

He thrust, shoving his slick length in.

"Corbin," I moaned around the stab of pain and pleasure, which had me groaning dirty and low.

"Fuck, my boy. You're so tight around me. Want to stay inside you all the time."

Whimpering, I pushed back against his hips, wanting him to move. "Live in there all you want, but move, Daddy, please."

His hands smoothed up and down my spine, my back and shoulders. "My good little cockslut, pleading for more. And since you've been good, I'll give you what you want."

He slowly pulled out, just leaving the tip teasing my rim. I heard him squirt some more lube out and wondered what my mate was up to, but quickly found out when he pressed a thumb into my hole along with his cock.

We both groaned.

"Hell, boy. Fuckin' love your ass." His free hand slapped down on a cheek before he fucked me with his cock and thumb.

I pressed my forehead into the bed, eyes rolled back, mouth gaping when he kept stabbing at my button.

So good, so good, so good.

"Daddy," I whimpered, already feeling the tingle.

"Hold on, sunshine." He removed his thumb and gripped my hips, drilling into me harder and faster.

"Daddy Sir."

"Hold on," he demanded.

I reached for my cock to strangle the end, trying to stop the fast-approaching climax.

Corbin leaned down, nipped at my shoulder. "Already imagin' my name on you, baby. Fuckin' got my balls tightenin'. Gonna fill you up and we're gonna rest with my cum still in you before I drain your cock again with my mouth."

"Daddy," I whined on a choked breath.

"Ready, boy. Come for me while I fill your tight hole."

Stars dance behind my lids as I yelled through my release over his sheets, and I felt the warmth of his seed splashing my walls.

Corbin pulled out, got onto the bed, and lay me over him. Our heavy breaths mixed with each other's. His hand slid down and cupped my ass, tightening around the globe.

"Best lay I've ever had—" I rose up to snarl until he added, "Probably because I love the hell outta you, Riker. You were damn made for me and I'm glad I took you from that club when I did. Wouldn't want to be anywhere else. Wouldn't want anyone else."

Smiling, I snuggled into his chest and patted there. "Love you too, Daddy Sir."

CHAPTER FOURTEEN

CORBIN

I jolted awake when someone pounded on the door. Riker was up in a crouch, growling, until he realized where he was. He slumped to his knees and rubbed at his eyes with the heels of his palms.

Christ, he was cute.

Sitting, I dragged him down with me and flicked the covers back over his body in case someone was stupid enough to walk in without my saying so.

"What?" I clipped loudly.

"Got a situation, Prez," Coms said through the door.

"Be down soon."

"Better hurry. Writer's makin' a scene about findin' cameras in his room."

"Got it," I called, and then muttered, "Fuck." I swiped

a hand over my face and used the other to tap Riker's perky ass. "Up, sunshine."

He kissed my pec and jumped out of bed, full of beans already.

"Thought you'd be sore, boy," I said.

We'd fucked another two times since we couldn't get enough of each other and then talked about a bit of everything before we showered in the early hours and crashed.

I pulled my sluggish body out of the bed, watching Riker getting dressed like he'd been awake for hours. I was sure we only got a few minutes of sleep.

"Oh, I am sore, but I love knowing how much you wanted my hole."

"Always."

He beamed. "Good." He skipped over to me as I finished doing up my jeans and picked up a tee. On his tiptoes, he puckered, and I chuckled but bent to meet his lips. "I need food before I get hangry."

"Can't have you hangry, sunshine. Never know who you'll stab."

His eyes widened. "You get me." He rushed over to the door while I slipped on my cut over my tee.

"Shoes?" I asked, putting my socks and boots on.

He cocked his head to the side. "Do I have to?"

Grinning, I shook my head. He'd already told me he liked being naked, and if he couldn't do that, he wanted bare feet in any place he could. Except on jobs.

He blew me a kiss, opened the door, and raced out.

"Riker," I called.

"Food," he called. "You wore me out last night and

you promised there are always meals available. I want to see what they've got." He raced off without me.

Snorting, I closed my door and made my way down to the common room. When I entered, I quickly noted there were no women around and not all brothers lingered, though the room was still busy.

Writer jumped up from a chair at one of the tables when he saw me.

"Sit the fuck down," Spade roared.

"But—"

"Shut it," I ordered.

"I've been here longer than you, boy—"

"Don't call me boy," I snarled, striding up to where he still stood. "Your VP told you to sit the fuck down. Do it."

"I'm too old for this shit. I'm outta—"

"Try to leave and you won't get far." I stepped closer. "Sit. The fuck. Down."

Writer plonked down with a scowl, but I caught his gulp and the sweat beading over his brow. I wasn't sure why he hadn't run already when he found the cameras, but more fool to him for not trying. Even though we would've collected him soon after he left.

The kitchen door at the far end of the room opened and Riker strolled out holding a tray full of food and drinks. He stared down at it hungrily.

I turned from Writer, so he didn't see my smitten smile. Riker ignored everything going on and all the people gawking at him to sit further down the table to eat.

Monkey snorted. "Never seen a man run to a kitchen faster than him." He clasped me on the shoulder. "Must'a been a good night."

Scowling, I told him, "It ain't any of your business."

Monkey grinned.

I ignored him and faced Writer again. "Tell me your side."

Writer's brows pinched. "What do you mean? I found cameras hidden in my room and want to know what fucker thought to play a trick on me." He peered off. "Was it you, Coms? This because I got your pussy?" He laughed and looked around for others to join in. When no one did, he went on, "She don't want a youngin' like you. She wanted someone who knows what—"

"Enough," I bit out.

"Man, you're not this stupid," Spade said with a shake of his head.

"What're you talkin' about?" Writer asked.

"You know why the cameras were in your room."

He tensed. "I don't."

Sighing, I ran a hand over my head. "You think we wouldn't check into things when Pauly called Spade about the missin' payment? Trusted you, brother. But can I really call you a brother now?"

"I haven't done anythin'."

"Says a person who's guilty," Monkey voiced. "Looked into the books, Writer. Saw some miscalculations."

The brothers around us started cursing and saying shit as they gathered closer. They silenced as soon as I raised a hand.

"I haven't done—"

"Lie to me again and I won't be fuckin' happy. Why you takin' from club businesses? What you need the extra money for?"

It'd better be a good answer.

His jaw clenched as he lowered his gaze to the floor.

"I was in this club with your pops. With your dad. You gonna do this shit to me in front of everyone? Where's the respect?"

"Respect? You wanna talk about respect? We trusted you and you shit all over that by takin' money from the club. Takin' money from your family. It doesn't matter you knew my pops and that crackhead of a father. I'm the one who brought this club outta its hellhole after dad ran it into the ground. You came to me, Writer, and told me I'd done a good job. That Pops would be happy. That we can live a clean, good life with the brotherhood again. When did things go wrong for you, Writer? When did you turn your back on the brotherhood and betray us?"

He glanced to the exit. I braced. If he was foolish enough to try and run, I'd take him down.

A sigh left him, and his shoulders drooped. The fight in him vanished.

He shook his head and ran a hand over his withered face.

"Cards," he said.

"Gamblin'?" Coms asked.

He nodded.

"You stole from your family for an addiction of bettin'?" Monkey demanded.

"You don't understand. I won big and I can do it again. I just need more time."

Fucking hell.

Disappointment coated my insides.

"You're cut from the club. We'll sell your house to pay

us back and leave you with a good amount to start over somewhere that ain't this town."

He jumped up. "What? No, you can't fuckin' do this."

"It was your choice to cheat your brothers outta money. It was your choice to keep doin' it to aid an addiction that we could've helped you out of."

"Harper won't be with me if—" He clamped his lips closed.

I closed the distance between us. "Harper? Did she get in your ear and tell you it was a good idea to take from us?"

"No."

"Do not fuckin' lie to me," I roared in his face.

A chair scraped, and I flicked my gaze over to see that Riker stood, knife in hand.

Drawing in a breath, I took a step back and shook my head his way while I asked Writer, "Tell me about you and Harper." I crossed my arms over my chest and waited.

"I'm just helpin' her out at the moment. She's been stayin' with me after she got fired from her job."

This was bullshit. Yeah, it was his addiction in the first place that caused him to fuck us over. But it was probably her that encouraged him to keep going or to get more than he'd needed.

We'd find out. I shot a look to Coms. He nodded and ducked out of the room.

"Then it looks like she'll have'ta find a new place too."

"Don't do this, Razor. I've been in the club for decades. You can't just throw me out like a piece of trash because of an addiction."

"That's what cuts me the most, Writer. That you've been with the club for decades, so you know that we would've helped you through your addiction. Instead, you chose to go behind our backs and deceive us." I ground my teeth together. "Take off your cut and leave. Pack your shit at the house and get outta town. Coms will be in touch when we sell your joint. And don't ever fuckin' forget you'll be watched, so it's time to make smart choices."

He flinched and deflated.

He didn't have a leg to stand on. He'd fucked up when he'd screwed us over and taken money from the club. We sat pretty well above the green line in our lives. None of the brothers struggled. He wouldn't have been either. Until his addiction grew and was probably fed on from some pussy who kept his dick wet.

No bitch was worth losing the club over.

No *addiction* was worth losing the club over.

My situation was different. I wasn't losing the club. I was stepping away for the man I loved with my whole goddamn soul.

"Fuck, brother," Writer said.

"Not your brother any longer. Remove the cut. Tanker, Grenade, and Jaws will escort you to the house to pack and then outta the area. You know what will happen if we see you around. If we get wind of you scramblin' for any type of revenge against the club."

He nodded, slipping his cut from his shoulders, and dropping it to the table.

"Nothin' I can say that'd help the situation." He was right. There wasn't.

"Hope you get help, so you don't fuck anyone else over," I told him. My gut rolled with unease over the whole damn matter. We would have helped him. All he had to do was reach out to anyone in the brotherhood.

Writer's jaw clenched. He tipped his chin up at me and walked from the room with the brothers I'd appointed as his watch, following him.

Arms wound around my waist, and I looked down to a softly smiling Riker. "I got you a coffee and some food. Might be a bit cold now, though." His nose scrunched. "I can get you fresh stuff."

Dipping down, I pressed a kiss to his forehead. "I'm good, sunshine. I'll take what you already got."

"You sound sad," he whispered.

"Just disappointed, sunshine. He was a good brother before he chose his addiction over his family."

He glided a finger over my brows, which I knew were tight from stress. "Do you want me to hurt anyone?"

Christ, he really is my cute, little psychopath shifter.

Pride and love flooded my veins. This man would do anything for me.

Cupping the back of his head, I threaded my fingers into his soft locks and dragged him up to meet my mouth.

Some of the brothers shouted their mild teasing or went crazy with catcalls and whistles.

I ignored them all. All I wanted to do was to devour him in more ways, but I still had shit to deal with.

CHAPTER FIFTEEN

RIKER

I really wanted to punch someone. Better yet, I'd like to slice a certain person's body until their blood coated the floor around us. It was Writer. I wanted him in pain since he was the one who put that frown on my mate's mouth. At least, before he'd kissed me. I'd wiped his frown away and he'd started smiling for me.

I was magic.

A real wizard at getting my mate to smile and I liked that I had that power.

I also loved that he kissed me again in front of his family.

His hands squeezed my ass cheeks, causing my spent cock to perk up like a dog did when its owner showed them a bone.

Corbin was my owner. I'd do anything he asked of me.

Anything.

He broke the kiss and rested his forehead to mine. "Got some business to still deal with, sunshine."

I tipped my chin up and pouted when he straightened. "Come and eat first."

His gaze ran over my face, and I dropped my lower lip some more. I wanted to feed my mate. I could hear he was hungry.

He rolled his eyes, smirked, and slapped my ass. "Fine."

Someone scoffed. "You really gonna kick Writer out, claim his possessions, and let this freak order you around because you like stickin' it in his shithole?"

"It's fuckin' sick. Never thought you'd turn into a pansy, Razor. Maybe it's you who needs to leave."

For a beat, I stilled.

"Riker," Corbin warned low.

Slowly, I smiled and turned my eyes the way the voices came from.

"Fuck." His hand fisted my hair, ripping my head back. My mouth opened, and I panted out my breath as our gazes locked. I could *feel* the desire rising in both of us, but I could also scent it from my mate.

Grinning, I then licked my lips.

"I've got this," he told me.

"No one disrespects you."

"I'll handle it, and you can have your chance when I allow it, Riker."

"What the fuck?" someone muttered.

Another snorted. "I ain't afraid of a tiny homo."

"You'd be a fuckin' fool then," Spade said, which

made me like the guy that little bit more. I hoped he went to Soren's other club. Not the one that Corbin met me at, but the one on the card. His sexy-time club. Soren would blow Spade's mind, which he deserved after having my back. I'd have to tell Soren to be extra attentive to him.

Corbin tensed, dropped his hold on me and turned to the room. "Spade, call all brothers in. I'm gonna sit the fuck down and eat breakfast, and *then*, we're all gonna have a word."

"You got it, Prez." Spade got his phone out and walked from the room while typing away.

My mate ignored the fools who'd said something and came for me, gripping the back of my neck and leading us back to where I'd been sitting. He pulled out a chair, sat, and tugged me down onto his lap.

"Riker?"

I dragged my attention away from glaring around the room to him. "Yes?" I asked, smiling sweetly.

"Feed me, boy."

A shiver rolled through me. "Okay," I whispered, dragging the tray over. I scowled down at the cold food and drink. "You need warm stuff."

"You got it for me. I'll eat it."

"Can I get you more? Please?"

Grinning, he pulled me against him and kissed me. "If it makes you happy, go for it."

I jumped up from his lap and picked up the tray. "Won't be long." I walked into the kitchen and saw Legless still cooking at the stove. He'd helped me before, so I was sure he'd give me more. I emptied the cold stuff in the bin and went over to stand beside him.

He did a double take when he noticed me. "Didn't you eat enough before?"

"This is for Corbin. His stuff went cold because he was dealing with business. By the way, they'll be a meeting soon to talk about Writer who was stealing from the club." I froze, except for my eyes widening. "I'm not sure if I was supposed to say that."

Legless chuckled. "Relax, kid. I heard the yellin' all the way in here."

"Oh. Okay." I smiled as he grabbed me a clean plate and placed some bacon and eggs on there. "The meeting will also be about Corbin and me. I don't think he likes some of his men saying stuff about him and me together. I mean, I know it's hard to accept for some people, but I just can't understand why, in this day and age, people can't just let others love who they want. It's not harming them. Okay, maybe we need to keep the touching and kissing to the bedroom so it's not in their faces, but can't they be happy for their boss?" I cocked my head to the side and looked at Legless instead of the food he'd put on the tray I held. "Unless you don't like same-sex relationships? Are me and Corbin going to be a problem for you?" I lifted the tray and sniffed the food. I didn't scent any poison.

"What are you doin'?"

"Smelling for poison."

"You can smell that?"

"Yes." There was no tang to this meal.

He snorted. "To answer your question, and so you don't have to check all the food I cook, I don't give a shit who's in who. Happiness is the key to life, kid. You and the prez have found it. A lotta the brothers can see the change in the prez and think it's damn awesome. Gotta make sure to keep what you two are creatin', and fuck anyone who says otherwise. Kiss, hug, and hell, fuck in front of anyone you want. This is Razor's place. He runs it. He brought most of us in, so he can do what he wants. They'll only be a few who don't like seein' anythin', but all they gotta do is look or walk the other way." He huffed. "I'd be pissed too if the people I trusted spoke shit to my partner."

"You're a nice guy, Legless."

He chuckled. "Kid, it's Reckless."

Oops. "Sorry," I offered with a grin.

"All good. Go get a cuppa joe for the prez."

"Will do. And you let me know if you need anyone killed. I'll do it." I balanced the tray on one hand and patted his arm before I went to the coffee machine and got a mug of hot coffee for my mate.

I took the tray out into the common room, which was fuller than before, and sat back on Corbin's lap. Though, he was now surrounded by others.

He tucked me close and kissed my shoulder. "Thanks, sunshine."

"You're welcome." I curled an arm around his shoulders, and as he talked to his brothers, he ate. Satisfaction filled me at seeing Corbin devour the food.

Reckless was right. I only noted a few of Corbin's men glaring at us. The rest were either listening to Corbin, Monkey, and Spade talking or having their own conversations. They didn't look at us with disdain in their gazes.

There was a scuffle down the hallway, and I heard

Coms saying, "Quit movin' like that, bitch." He entered with a grip on Harper's upper arm, and she kept trying to pull free.

Corbin tapped my ass. I stood and moved in behind him when he scooted his chair back to face their approach.

"What the fuck is this, Razor?" Harper snapped.

I wanted to stab her in the throat for her tone and her nasty, scrunched-up face.

Corbin stood. "Brothers, let it be known that Harper is no longer allowed in our club."

"You can't," she screeched, tugging on her arm again to move toward Corbin.

I wished he'd let her. Grinning, I rocked on my feet, ready to take her down if she even tried to touch him.

Corbin glowered down at her. "I can and I will." He addressed the room again. "She's banned from here, from speakin' to any member, from touchin' any member."

Brothers grunted, shouted, or nodded their acknowledgment.

"Means the other women here, too, Harper," Spade added. "You stay away from them."

She laughed. "You think the brothers will want to give this up?" She grabbed her crotch. "They won't listen—"

"Bitch, we only put up with you for Writer's sake," Reckless called. "You been tryin' for other brothers for a while, but did anyone take you up on the offer? We don't stick it in toxic bitches."

The brothers agreed in their own way while Harper glanced all around her with a sour face.

"Yeah, well, Writer still wants me." She placed her attention back on Corbin for a beat before it slid to me standing at his side. "He's going to make me his old lady. I'm not going anywhere."

Laughing, I tucked my chin down and looked up at her. "Writer is no more."

She shifted away. "What do you mean?"

Corbin explained, "He's been kicked out of the club for the money he stole. Money you no doubt encouraged him to take. The club's sellin' his place for repayment. In fact, he's there now packin' up."

She tore her arm away and stormed toward Corbin.

Red coated my vision.

I rushed her and took her to the ground with my hand around her throat. It wasn't hard and I didn't bang her down. Just surprised her with my speed and action so she, more or less, fell with my guiding. I didn't harm women—unless it was necessary and in a life-and-death situation.

My fox and I growled in her ear.

She never would have heard that sound from a human.

She stilled and stared up at me as if I was a monster as I slowly pulled away.

I was.

"You'll do as he says. You'll stay away from everyone associated with the club or I'll come for you and when I do, I won't be easy on you, Harper. I'll take my time and make sure you suffer for messing with my man."

Pulling back, I peered into her eyes with my fox.

Then I jumped up and brushed my hands together, walking back to Corbin.

The room was silent. I didn't know why. They'd seen

me defend before when that dirtbag touched one of my friends. What was different this time?

Corbin curved his arm around my shoulders when I wrapped mine around his waist and tucked myself into his side. He dipped down to kiss my forehead. I winked up at him.

"No blood."

"You did good, sunshine."

I preened at his words and snuggled closer.

Harper kept her mouth closed as she got to her feet.

"Looks like Harper got the message," Spade said, his tone light with humor.

She sent him the middle finger.

"Prank, grab a brother and escort Harper off our property to Writer's so she can pack."

Her gaze flashed wide for a moment.

Corbin must have seen it, he said, "Yeah, we know you were livin' with him. You'll get some cash to help you find a place. But don't ever come back here for anythin'. No one will help you. Hear me?"

When she stayed quiet, I moved out of Corbin's arms.

"I hear you," she said quickly before she turned and walked out with some men following her.

"Wish that was all the business we had to talk about, but it ain't," Corbin announced. "For those who don't know, but probably figured, Writer was skimmin' off our books." Voices rose but stopped when Corbin's hand shot up again. "He's not a brother any longer. No one is to communicate with him or Harper. If you do, there'll be consequences."

No one said a word.

"Coms, take note of what we're about to talk about," he ordered.

Coms tipped his chin up and pulled out his phone.

My mate looked tired even though we hadn't been awake for long. We didn't get much sleep, and I doubt he had any regrets about that, but I would make sure he got enough sleep in the future, so he had enough energy to deal with annoying matters.

Before he sat down on his seat again, he leaned the back of it up against the table to face everyone. I picked my spot on the floor, leaning against his leg. His hand cupped the back of my neck.

"Shouldn't we be doin' this meetin' in church for just members?" someone called, but I recognized the butthead as the same man who called Corbin a pansy.

"You talkin' about Riker bein' here, Marker?"

Marker.

Huh, suited him because I'd put a marker on him, and he'd soon be dead if he caused any more stress to my mate.

I looked up to Corbin. "I can go to the bedroom."

Marker scoffed, and his friend who'd also said something before snorted. Marker shook his head. "Yeah, be a good whore and—*Oof.*" He glared at Monkey who'd punched him in the gut. "What'd you do that for?"

"Learn to shut the hell up, you fucker, and respect the prez's partner."

"A guy?" he spluttered, straightening. "You can't be serious with a guy."

"What's wrong with it?" Coms asked.

"It ain't right. That's what's wrong," Marker replied.

"Yeah, it's disgustin'," his asshole friend added.

"You'll just agree with anythin' Marker says, Boff," another called.

"That's exactly what I wanted to talk about," Corbin said, and the room quieted. Big boss man, *my man*, was pissed. He near vibrated from the anger burning in his gaze. "If anyone has an issue with how I lead my life, who I share my bed with, my heart with, then you can fuck off from the club. I ain't puttin' up with anyone disrespectin' Riker in any way. But also, that bigotry shit can fuck right off outta here. Thought we'd be above that. Thought we lived like we wanted and without a care, but here I am being judged by my own brothers because I fell in love with a man. A man who has had my back in everythin'."

"You're pickin' a guy you fuck over your brothers?" Marker said, upper lip rising.

"Fuck, you're stupid," Spade clipped. "He's pickin' a man who he damn loves. Has anyone seen our prez as happy as he has been in the last few days before?" No one replied. "Exactly. And you dickheads wouldn't have a problem with Prez's relationship if it was with a woman. Get over it and yourselves. I'm in with Prez. If anyone has a problem with same-sex relationships within the club, then leave. Who's with me?"

There were shouts and a lot of cussing that ran around the room. The only two who were still and silent, looking at all of us with an upturned nose, were Marker and Boff.

My heart boomed in my chest with fondness for the other men who supported their boss man and me. I already knew I'd kill for them, but if they needed anything other than murdering, I'd be willing to help them out.

Except those two fools.

"Fuck this, I'm out. I ain't sittin' around to witness this sickenin' shit. Our president who's wrapped up in a little fuckin' faggot who's insane—" Marker snapped his mouth closed and tried to back up, but the brothers held him in place as Corbin approached. "Wait, wait, wait," Marker chanted.

Corbin fisted the front of his vest and tee and lifted him. "Say what you want about me, but I've had enough of you talkin' about Riker like that." He dropped him hard so that Marker fell on his ass. He stalked back to Spade and held out his hand. Spade produced a blade and gave it over to Corbin.

My body tingled.

My cock jerked.

I licked my dry lips and watched in awe as my mate crouched in front of Marker.

"Hold him," he ordered, and his men complied. "You shoulda just had your say and picked to stay or leave, but you just had to open your mouth and say shit about the man I love. For that, you get to remember where you fucked up."

Marker begged and yelled as Corbin took his hand, held it flat on the floor, and sliced his finger off.

I grinned.

Corbin stood. "I don't see either of you changin' your ways in thinkin'. Not askin' for it either. Would rather be done with you two. Take off your cuts before you leave. Pick wisely in your future, because if you come back for us in any way, I'll end you."

Monkey leaned down and pressed a gun to Marker's head. "You heard my prez, right?"

Marker nodded, holding his hand to his chest. Boff helped him up and they removed their vests. Someone took the items from them before they started for the door.

"We'll be watchin'," Reckless called.

"No one fucks with Fury MC!" someone shouted, and a roar went up around the room.

CHAPTER SIXTEEN

CORBIN

I walked back over to Riker, pulled him close with my fingers through his hair, and slammed my mouth down on his. The brothers had my back, so did my sunshine. Plus, we'd got rid of those who were going to be a problem. If they popped up in the future, we'd take care of them again.

Pride had me breaking the kiss and looking around at my brothers.

All of them supported my choice. Even after throwing the surprise of my new relationship in their faces, they showed that their loyalty was thicker than those other bigoted cunts.

"Thank you, brothers. Know it's early, but I'm declaring a damn party day. Stock the shelves, bring in the women. It's time to celebrate livin'."

More cheering arose.

I'd enjoy all the days I could with the club. Until I handed it over to Spade. Until Riker and I moved with the family and put down roots in a different place.

No matter where we were, though, I'd keep an eye on the club. If they ever needed help, I'd find a way to do it.

They were my family, no matter where I would be in the world.

Riker wiggled against me. "Even though I wanted to gut them, I liked watching you take care of that annoying issue. You were smoking hot. Not that you're not all the time. You are." He nodded. "All. The. Time."

Chuckles sounded around us.

"We get it, Riker. You think the prez is hot," Spade said.

"All the time," Monkey added.

More laughter rang out.

At least I knew from Riker's wide grin, he didn't want to kill them for their teasing.

It's gonna be a good day.

Cupping his ass, I lifted him into my arms as I sat so he could straddle my waist. A brother dropped off a couple of drinks for us, but Riker wouldn't touch his. He didn't need it to have a good time. He was pure sunshine already. All he needed was a conversation or a smile and he could switch in a blink of an eye. Loved that about him. Loved a fucking lot about the man in my arms.

He turned to Spade as my brother said, "Aww, look at the lovebirds."

"Don't be jealous, Spade. You'll find our kind of love one day."

"I hope so, kid. I do."

The doors opened and the women entered. Riker kissed me quick and jumped up.

"Got to go talk to my posse. Drink, get merry, and I'm sure I'll enjoy the reward from it later." He winked and skipped off.

"Hell, Prez, I'm definitely seein' the appeal. He's sweet to look at, violent, fast, possessive, and kind," Coms commented.

I huffed. I liked that my brothers were seeing Riker for the deadly and sweet person he was, but still.... "Don't look too long there, brother, or I'll have to cut your eyes out."

Maybe.

It was possible.

If he really pissed me off.

Let's hope that doesn't happen.

RIKER

I mouthed at Corbin's neck, where his tattoo of my fox and pet name lay. I sat on his lap in his office at the compound with my ass half hanging off so his fingers could play with my hole. He either pushed in and out, pressed against my button, or toyed with my rim. All while he did some paperwork.

He was driving me insane. But he liked teasing me to the edge.

I enjoyed it too. Enjoyed knowing he found pleasure in his leisurely actions. In controlling me in ways where it slowed my thoughts and actions.

He was a master at knowing what I needed and when.

It hadn't even been six months and he pulled at my strings like he was a seasoned violinist.

Our time so far had been crazy, wild, and fun.

I thought I'd been happy living with my brothers and giving them hell before I met him.

But I hadn't really known what happiness was until my amazing, perfect fated mate rushed into my life and swept me off my feet.

I loved waking up and going to sleep with him. I loved taking him on jobs. Which I'd had the chance to a few times, and he'd been wet-dream amazing in those situations where I wanted to drop to my knees and suck him off.

But my brothers would have frowned upon that.

Boring.

I nipped at his neck, needing his attention. "Daddy Sir," I whimpered.

He dropped his pen and gave me his burning gaze as he inserted his fingers inside and scissored them. I fisted his tee.

"Fuck, boy. I love your ass."

I sucked at his neck. "Hmm, I know."

"Could play with it all the time."

Laughing, I kissed where I'd marked. "You do."

"You make me greedy, sunshine. But I'm in need of somethin' else right now." He pulled his fingers free, pushed his chair back, and ordered with a tip of his chin, "To your knees."

I slipped down between his spread legs and licked my lips as he undid his jeans.

"Gonna come on your face, boy. Need to paint you with my scent, rub it in so you reek of it."

Nodding, I crawled forward and rested my hands on

his thick thighs. He reached in and pulled his hard, leaking cock out.

"Already close, boy. Playin' with you turns me on." He stroked up and down his length, eyes running up and over me. "Stick your tongue out. Need you waitin' for my cum. But want you to touch yourself, sunshine."

My mouth watered, but I stuck my tongue out and lifted my ass off my calves to shove my shorts down. Resting back on my shins, I spread my knees a little and inserted two fingers in my wet hole. I used my other hand to wrap around my aching cock.

Moaning, I fucked myself and watched, waiting for my mate's load. Knew it'd splash on my tongue and skin in a warm release so I would draw it all over my face and neck.

I stopped to remove my tee so I could glide it down over my chest and then went back to playing with myself. Gaze stuck on my mate's hand working his cock over and over.

Even if we didn't shower before dinner at home with my brothers, I didn't care they'd know what we'd done. Why I reeked. They were just as bad with their mates as I was with mine.

Corbin and I couldn't stop touching and loving each other.

We never ran out of things to talk about either.

We ate, drank, watched movies, played cards, and billiards at both the compound and home. We teased, laughed, and just cherished all our time together.

His brothers always joked about us being glued to one another, and it was true. I never wanted to be far from him. I always wanted his hands on me. And I revelled in the fact that he was mine for as long as we lived.

My stomach swirled, my balls tightened, and a tingle raced down my spine.

"Daddy, I'm close," I whimpered.

"Good boy, so am I." He moved his ass forward on his seat, gaze flicking over me. From my hand jerking my cock to my arm that moved my fingers in and out as I played with my hole. I loved the obscene sounds it made from how wet my daddy sir had already gotten it.

Bitting on my bottom lip, I watched Daddy's tip leak and drop down to the floor. I wanted to lick the end, suck on it, but I wished for his cum to splash over my face and body more.

Especially when Daddy Sir got that burning look in his eyes.

Like he hungered for me.

Like he wanted to mark me.

Like he owned me.

And he did.

I was his all the time.

"Christ, boy, you're gorgeous." His hand sped up.

I whimpered. My body throbbed with arousal.

"Daddy," I whispered.

"Tongue out again," he ordered.

I stuck my tongue out and leaned forward. Fucking my hole, I made sure to rub at my button faster, harder.

My cock squirted out its release at the first touch of Daddy's cum warming my face, neck, shoulders, and chest.

He groaned low and then snarled, "Fuck." I rubbed

his seed into my cheek, over my lips, in my mouth where I sucked on the fingers until I dipped back out to glide the rest over my skin.

Closing my eyes, I moaned. His scent was everywhere and so strong, it had my head buzzing and my cock trying to perk up while my ass tightened around nothing.

I wanted him again.

Opening my eyes, I dragged my top teeth over my bottom lip, watching his scorching gaze on me.

"Daddy," I uttered.

His upper lip rose in a silent snarl before he threaded his fingers in my hair and dragged me forward, slamming his lips down on mine. Kissing and biting, we licked at each other's mouths.

He pulled me up to stand between his legs, still kissing me as he fixed my shorts.

"If we didn't promise Rio we'd be home for dinner, I'd take you upstairs and fuck you hard, boy."

Smiling, I said, "I don't mind being late."

His chuckle was sweet to hear, like every time he did it. He stood, drawing me into him. "But I don't want a quick fuck, sunshine. Wanna take my time eatin' you before I fill you with my cum again."

A shiver raked over me, and my belly tingled. "Then let's get home for dinner so we can get to dessert."

"Go grab another tee and I'll meet you at our rides."

I glanced down at my other tee on the floor and saw it had his spunk on it. "I'll just wear—"

"Riker, tee, and wash a little. Only a little. Can't be too disrespectful at the dinner table. Especially when your mom's gonna be there."

I cocked my head to the side. "Are you sure? Mom won't care, and my brothers are just as bad as us. I could smell Nox all over and *in* Kieran in the office the other day, and this morning, Rio's breath reeked of Deacon's—" His hand covered my mouth.

"Love you. But I don't need to know about them and when they stink of sex, yeah?"

Cackling, I nodded. "You got it and love you too." I gave him a quick kiss before I picked up my tee and rushed from the room.

On the way to our bedroom, I spotted Spade in the common room. "Have fun tonight," I called. Corbin had told me he was going to check out Soren's club. He wasn't sure if he'd sleep with Soren yet, but he didn't know how persuasive that vampire could be. Either way, they'd have fun. I was sure of it.

And wouldn't it be totally cool if Spade was Soren's fated mate. The only way they'd find out was if Soren drank from him. Vampires couldn't scent their mates like shifters. It was even harder for fae. They discovered if they had a fated when an identical tattoo seared into both of their bodies. But that was only if they were close by each other... like in the same building.

Spade grinned and tipped his chin my way.

"Hey, sugar," Lynette said, coming through the door I was about to exit. She snorted. "I can see you've been having fun. Got a bit of something on your neck."

Snickering, I rubbed more of Corbin in. "Thanks. Gotta wash a little before we head home for dinner with the family. You here to see Reckless again?" My girl had a major crush on our cook. He was slowly seeing how awesome she was.

Not as good as Corbin, though. No one could be.

She smiled. "Maybe. But I want to know when you're going to bring these brothers in?"

"Probably never. They're a little possessive of their guys, and if a brother looked at either of them wrong, my brothers will kill them."

"So, they're like you?"

Snorting, I shook my head and playfully pushed her gently. I didn't want her body to go flying if I used all my strength. It'd be a shame to see her body go splat into the wall.

"I haven't killed anyone in the club. Yet."

"Yet, you say." Laughing, she caught sight of Reckless as he walked out of the kitchen. "I'm feeling kind of hungry."

"Oh, I know that hunger. Go get him, sweet pea." As she walked by, I slapped her on the ass. I only did it because Corbin wasn't bothered by mine and Lynette's friendship. He thought it was cute how I'd taken all the women in the club under my legs. Besides, he knew I was completely his in every way.

I quickly went to our room, washed at record speed, dressed, and raced outside to where my mate waited for me as he sat astride his ride. I climbed on the back and placed on the helmet he gave me.

"Ready, Daddy Sir," I called, wrapping my arms around his waist. Well, they were nearly all the way around. He was a big man after all.

Corbin ran his hand along my arm and held mine to

his stomach. It was his way of telling me to hold on tight before we set off.

I had, on many occasions, offered to take my own bike. But my Corbin liked having me close. Liked knowing he could reach for me if anything happened.

He also got a wee angry when we had gone riding and I'd taken a few corners at crazy speeds. I got my ass tanned good and proper that night. It'd been awesome. But I also didn't like worrying my daddy, so I stuck to being a passenger. I liked being hugged up to him too.

When we pulled into the garage a short while later, I could already smell dinner cooking.

I jumped off and placed my helmet on the rack to the wall. An arm wound around my chest and lips touched down to my neck as Corbin put his next to mine.

He took my hand and pulled me along toward the kitchen. I liked to linger behind, enjoying seeing my smaller hand in his big tattooed one. It warmed my belly each and every time, like it was now.

"Hey," Corbin called as we entered.

"Hi." I grinned.

"You two reek," Nox said.

"Leave them be," Mom said as she hugged us both quickly.

"Where's Grey?" I asked. He was Mom's fella, who we'd come to accept and love.

"He'll be by later. Busy with work."

"Dinner's nearly ready," Rio said.

"Riker, set the table," Deacon ordered.

"*Please*," Corbin added, gripping the back of my tee when I made to move over there.

Deacon's jaw clenched. My mate and oldest brother had a love-hate relationship. But I knew one day it would turn into a buddy friendship. Nox was just an ass to everyone but Kieran, so I didn't bother worrying about him getting along with Corbin. Still, Nox liked him enough not to kill him and accept his help on jobs.

Through clenched teeth, Deacon said, "Riker, please set the motherfucking table. Right now."

"I can do it," Kieran put in, our peacekeeper, but Nox curled an arm around him, holding his mate in his chair as he watched on with a smirk.

Corbin's upper lip rose, but he released his hold on me. I jumped at him, kissed him swiftly, and skipped over to the kitchen area. I gave a brief side hug to Rio, and even Deacon, who grumbled under his breath but patted my back, and then I got what I needed. My mate helped me lay everything out because he was the sweetest man who ever graced my world.

By the time we were all seated and the food hit the table, my stomach howled in complaint.

Corbin took my plate from in front of me and piled the food on. I smiled up at him before I turned back to the others, listening and watching them. Mom was on the phone to Grey, telling him she'd leave him a plate. Nox dished up Kieran's food, as Deacon did Rio's. They smiled and talked softly to their mates.

All of us were the happiest we'd ever been.

All of us were content and in love.

My head was tugged back by my hair and Corbin growled, "What's this?" When he swiped at my cheek, I realized tears had fallen.

Grinning, I scooted onto his lap and hugged him tightly. "I'm just happy that we're all happy."

Corbin grunted, tightening his hold around my waist. "Okay then."

Kissing his neck, I went to slip off his legs, but he held me in place and pulled my plate close. I didn't mind staying right where I was. Even when Nox gagged and complained about how sickly cute we were. And Deacon rolled his eyes and shook his head. But I could tell they didn't really care because they were as lost as I was in our mates.

We truly were blessed with our fated mates, and we would do anything to protect what we treasured above anything. The ones who helped calm our hunger for blood and need to hunt.

But most of all, we would protect the ones who loved us and our animals unconditionally.

ACKNOWLEDGMENTS

To my readers who have read all the brothers' stories, thank you for loving them as much as I adored writing them.

Becky at Hot Tree Editing, thank you for all the help you do at making my work understandable. But for also fitting these novellas into your busy schedule.

Readers, you must check out her MM romances under the pen name: Becca Seymour.

    I also highly recommend MM authors: Louisa Masters, Saxon James, Eden Summers, Riley Hart, Sarah Honey, and Lisa Henry.

I am hoping to write more in this Protected series with books for Soren and Dash, but they'll probably come next year. For now, I'll be looking at writing my tortured soul: Torch. (if you know, you know).

ALSO BY L ROSE

Protected Series

Protected by the Bear Shifter

Protected by the Tiger Shifter

Protected by the Fox Shifter

The Hidden Kingdom Trilogy

(polyamorous)

A Torn Paige

A Lost Paige

A Final Paige

Standalone fantasy romance

Infinite Bond

(m/m/m/m)

Within the Darkness

(m/f/m/m)

Titles under Lila Rose

Hawks MC: Ballarat Charter

Holding Out (Free)

Outplayed (standalone related to the Hawks MC)

Climbing Out

Finding Out (novella)

Black Out

No Way Out

Coming Out (m/m novella)

Out to Find Freedom (standalone related to the Hawks MC)

Hawks MC: Caroline Springs Charter

The Secret's Out

Hiding Out

Down and Out

Living Without

Walkout (novella)

Hear Me Out (m/m)

Break Out (novella)

Fallout

Out of the Blue (standalone related to the Hawks MC: m/m/m)

Out Gamed (standalone related to the Hawks MC: novella)

Hawks MC: Next Generation

Coyote

Ruin (m/m)

Texas

Polished P & P Series (m/m romance)

Wreck Me Forever

Never a Saint

Working Out West

Diamond MC

Country

State (novella)

Death

Romantic Comedies

Making Changes

Making Sense

***

Fumbled Love

Bumbled Love